D0878167

Published by Fifth Avenue Publications.

Cover design by pro-ebookcovers

Edited by Indie Editing Chick

First Edition (July 2017)

Second Complete Edition (September 2017)

www.joslynwestbrook.com

CINDERELLA-ISH

Razzle My Dazzle Book One

JOSLYN WESTBROOK

THIS IS A LIMITED EDITION

Happy Reading!

Joslyn Westbrook

BLURB

PRINCE CHARMING CAN JUST SUCK IT...

Daniella Belle wants nothing more to do with members of the opposite sex; instead, she'll focus on what matters most—becoming a lingerie designer. That's until she's offered an opportunity of a lifetime by an annoyingly arrogant man who believes he can charm the panties off of every woman he meets.

Antonio Michaels has never had to work hard at anything. Born with a silver spoon in his mouth, he's been served up a hefty life of entitlement. He's handsome, charmingly arrogant, and dates a different model every month. When he meets Daniella Belle, a bombshell who seems unfazed by his mere existence, he finds himself captivated by her looks, her unrelenting potty mouth, and the fact he can't stop thinking about her.

Will Antonio have to work hard to make Daniella believe he's the man destined to sweep her off of her feet? Or will Daniella's bad luck with men make her continue to doubt fairytale romances truly exist?

DEDICATION

For Daryl...You Are My Prince Charming
Happy Anniversary Baby 🖤
"I Freaking Adore You, Damn It."

LOS ANGELES

"Los Angeles Fashion Is The Starbucks Of The Modeling World." -
Janice Dickinson

CHAPTER 1

DANIELLA

*Y*ou're a sweet, take-you-home-to-meet-my-mom type of a girl and I'm just not ready for something so serious.

The text message invades my phone like an unforeseen missile strike. Boom.

Is that the best Jacob Ryan could come up with? A pathetically buffed-up rendition of *it's not you, darling, it's me*?

A breakup text.

I've heard of them, yet seriously doubted I'd ever be on the receiving end of one.

You'd think I'd be hurt, right? Especially since Jacob and I've been dating for over a month. Forty-five days to be precise.

But I'm not hurt one bit.

Seriously.

I mean, I sort of gave up on meeting my *Prince Charming* ages ago. Mr. Charming does not exist and, believe me, every modern-day woman knows this, despite all of the sappy romance movies and novels out there.

So fuck it. I'm totally swearing off men now. Alpha men, hot men, poor men, rich men, short men, tall men…

Just men. Period. End of discussion.

And I mean it this time. I—Daniella Belle—do solemnly swear to *never* go out with another damn member of the opposite sex again. Ever.

Well, at least for now, anyway.

Never is a borderline extreme commitment that I'd surely fail to live up to. For example: Suppose Circa-2000 David Beckham were to strut across this busy Los Angeles Metro station platform wearing nothing except his ripped abs and jeans? He'd seductively squeeze his way through the crowd of downtown-bound commuters, his gaze glued to mine as he makes a beeline toward me, professing Victoria—what's-her-face—has left him and he wants to be with me. Then, of course, I'd forgo swearing off men.

Obviously.

Anyway, this epiphany-inducing text could not have come at a worse time. Today is *supposed* to be a great day. Yet already, my alarm clock failed to go off, I got shampoo in my eyes, there were no more Pop-Tarts in the pantry, and of course now, this gimpy-ass text.

When a day starts off bad, it has a tendency to only get worse. This theory has been statistically proven to be true, which instinctively compels me to internally pray to the good day gods that today does *not* snowball into an epic-fail-shit-happens sort of day. From this point on it's gotta be smooth mutha fuckin' sailing.

I'm on my way to a job interview that, if all goes as planned, will land me my dream job.

Well, my *almost* dream job. Let's just call this the get-my-foot-in-the-door-to-my-dream-job job. One that is, after all, the sole reason why I moved to Los Angeles from Dallas; to be a fashion designer—a designer of lingerie, to be more specific.

I graduated at the top of my class from LA's Fashion Institute of Design last year. Except so far, I've had zero luck getting anyone to notice my designs.

Budging my way through the crowd of busy Los Angeles commuters, I feel my phone's vibration through my purse.

I cringe.

It better not be another text from Jacob, the breakup texter.

I yank my phone out of my purse and peek at the caller ID.

Oh. It's my boss. Well, she's also a good friend. So what's the term for that? Boss slash friend?

"Hey, Stacy," I answer, slowly inching my way closer to the edge of the platform.

"Best of luck today, lovely. Have you caught the train yet?"

Stacy's actually the one who showed me the Google alert that mentioned: Antonio Michaels, Creator and CEO of *CraveMe Lingerie* is actively seeking a professional and experienced Personal Assistant.

Honestly, I had never even heard of Antonio Michaels. Sure I've heard of his *CraveMe* line of lingerie, but seriously… who hasn't?

"Not yet. Still waiting at the station. Along with a whole bunch of other people. I may have to fight my way onto the train." I laugh internally at my sarcasm.

"You can't be late for that interview. I don't want to lose you as a nanny to Emma, but you can't miss out on an opportunity so great."

True confession time: I've got no *real* experience being anyone's Personal Assistant; yet, Stacy swore that, since I've been a nanny to her daughter Emma, I've really been like her Personal Assistant over the past five years, basically keeping her entire professional world, as a lawyer, and personal world, as a single mom, organized.

Stacy helped me spruce up my résumé and gave me a respectable letter of recommendation. And a letter of recommendation from Stacy is full-on, drop-the-mic status, on account of she's a well-known entertainment lawyer.

"I won't miss the train. I promise. And thank you, Stacy. You're the best. Oh, and guess what? Jacob broke up with me." I pause and lower my voice after catching a woman in close proximity eavesdropping. "Via text," I add.

"What a loser!" Stacy announces as if it's breaking news. "I told you he doesn't deserve you. Anyway, I'm walking into court right now. Emma will be home briefly this afternoon before she heads to her dad's for the rest of the week."

I nod as if Stacy can see me.

"And I'm catching a red-eye to New York," she asserts.

I actually forgot about that. Even though I made all of her travel arrangements. She's off to some lawyers' convention for the week.

"Right. New York. Have fun!"

"Sure. Well, I'll catch up with you later. Good luck. Love ya."

"Love ya, too."

As the train approaches, I keep a careful eye out for anyone holding a coffee cup. The last thing I need is for someone to solidify this to be a bad day, by bumping into me and spilling coffee all over my new dress. Shit like that isn't just made for TV; it happens all the time.

The train reaches the platform and as soon as I board, I realize it's standing room only.

Figures.

These stilettos aren't really made for standing.

As I maneuver my way to the back of the train, hoping to find an empty seat, my phone buzzes.

Ugh. Another text from Jacob *the loser* Ryan.

Just checking: Did you get my text message this morning?

I roll my eyes in unbelievable disgust at his inquiry and am just about to text a scathing reply, letting him know exactly where he can shove his stupid-ass breakup text, when I trip over who knows what, and land right up against a tall, dark-haired guy who's eating—a jelly donut.

That's right a…Fucking. Jelly. Donut.

Never did I think I'd need to be on the lookout for anyone eating a fruity donut on the train. A donut that has left its explicit mark on the top half of the front of my brand-new sweater dress.

Did I mention it's a *white* dress?

"Whoops." The dark-haired guy snickers, as he continues to bite and annoyingly smack his way through his evil donut. He doesn't even look the least bit concerned with the fact that remnants of his shitty breakfast choice are now splattered across the top front of my dress as blatant as a large letter *S* for Superwoman.

I scoff at his nonchalant response and reach into my purse in search of something I can use to wipe off the massive glob of jelly.

"Whoops? That's all you've got to say?" I briefly consider getting my revenge by snatching what's left of the donut out of his hand and smearing it all over his light blue button-down dress shirt.

He produces a semi-wicked grin. "Well, it wasn't *my* fault. You do know you totally bumped into me, right? You really shouldn't be texting and walking. It's evidently impairing. In all actuality, I saved you."

I finally retrieve a tissue out of my purse. "I beg your pardon? You saved me?" I shake my head and roll my eyes. Surely he must know I'm annoyed.

"Yes. Had I not been standing here for you to clumsily bump into after you tripped, you would have epically face-planted your way to the floor of this train. So please…feel free to thank me anytime now."

Really? He can't possibly be serious, right? Where is this guy from: the land that time forgot?

"Oh, I'll thank you, alright. You, along with your fucking donut, have ruined my dress *and* my day. I'm on my way to a job interview. Now *this* is how I'll be presenting myself. So if anything, thank you for ruining my day."

The train gives a swift jolt as it takes off, and of course, the movement forces me into Mister Not-So-Friendly which, ironically causes part of the glob of jelly to rub off my dress and onto his shirt.

Pushing myself off of him, I grab a tight hold of the pole and can't help but laugh at the sight of his shirt.

Sweet ironic revenge at its best.

He looks down at his shirt, then up at me. Without taking his eyes off me, he swipes the jelly off his shirt with the tip of his index finger, and calmly licks the sticky goo before he winks. "I've got a wide selection of clean shirts I can change into at my office."

For a split second, the sight of him licking his finger makes my spine tingle. The dark-haired guy is scrumptiously gorgeous—tall, tan, with smoldering blue eyes. But his sarcastic remark just downright infuriates me.

"You're a first-class jerk, aren't you?" I suggest, feeling my face heat up.

"Why would you say such a thing? You hardly know me." The tone of his voice has a delicate accent to it, a sultry brew of American, Italian, and French—an international delight, perhaps.

"Thank goodness for that," I admit. "I would pay good money to never have to bump into the likes of you again."

"Ouch. You certainly do possess a spicy little bite, huh? And a huge scruffy attitude, too." He flirts as he runs his tongue across his soft lips.

I glare at him, displaying I'm not at all interested in flirtatious banter. "Scruffy attitude? Let's not forget *you* are a huge reason why I have this attitude."

He shakes his head. "Oh no. Don't try to pin it on me. I watched you as you got onto the train. You looked annoyed after you glanced at your phone. And now you're taking it out on me. Let me take a wild guess…did someone dump you via text?"

"You know what? Screw you!" I spit out, more shocked than he probably is. Sure, I tend to curse like a sailor, but not in the presence of hundreds of commuters on a train.

"Whoa! Such language for a little lady." He smiles conspiratorially leaning in close enough for me to get an accurate count of the somewhat sexy sprinkle of freckles along the bridge of his nose. "Tell me, how many guys have you kissed with that potty mouth of yours?"

I step back, flabbergasted at his blatant audacity to deliver such a question so bluntly. Without much thought, I cleverly toss back, "Tell me, how many women have you lost with that endless arrogance of yours? It spills out of you with as much force as water gushing out of a busted water main."

As the train comes to a halt I realize it's my stop. At least I think it is.

I rush past the brute who has un-graced me with his presence for the last ten minutes, and as I get closer to the exit, I hear his voice gripe in the distance. "Good luck on that job interview, Miss Potty Mouth. It's a crying shame you can't use me as your character reference."

I've walked at least three blocks and, thankfully, I'm just about there. I was so flustered on the train, I got off a stop too soon. But who could blame me? The guy was utterly despicable. In my not so humble opinion, walking the rest of the way is a winning trade-off, despite the fact I know darn well my feet are going to be done-in by these shoes once I get to the office building for the interview.

Part of me wants to head back to Stacy's Beverly Hills home and forget this interview since my appearance is less than to be desired. Honestly, who shows up to an interview with food spillage? My gut tells me something good has got to come out of this bad start to my day. The worst is behind me...left on that train.

When I finally arrive, with about twenty minutes to spare, I head straight for the receptionist desk to check in and when I approach, a young woman popping pink bubble gum is busy on the computer. She bops her head from side to side as if she's got a groovy pop song stuck in there. At first glance, it's safe for me to assume she's around my age—early twenties, at least. Her dark blue eyes switch from the computer screen to my face, then almost immediately switch to the pitiful stain on my dress.

"Oh. My. Goodness! What happened to your beautiful dress, hon?" She covers her mouth and her eyes widen, displaying what appears to be empathetic shock.

Instinctively, I try to cover the now dried-up jelly glob with the palm of my hand, but realize it's a total waste of time.

"Oh, I was accosted by a jelly donut on the train this morning," I sarcastically explain.

"A jelly donut? That's freakishly bizarre because—" She pauses, holds up her index finger, and mouths the words 'hold on', reaching to answer the office phone that sits underneath a pile of file folders on her desk.

As she diverts her attention to the person on the other end of the phone, I take a seat on one of the two couches that sits in the center of the lobby. The black-and-white walls are decorated with large gold-framed photos of women who are scantily adorned in exquisite lingerie pieces—a tasteful shrine of blown-up magazine spreads of *CraveMe* unmentionables.

"Sorry about the interruption," the woman says, with a gesture for me to make a return to her desk. "The phone has been ringing nonstop since a job opportunity was announced." She looks at me questionably. "Wait. Are you here for an interview?" She steals a quick glance at my ill-stained dress again.

"Yes, actually I am."

"Oh, goody! What's your name, hon?"

"Daniella Belle. Belle with an E." I anxiously tap my fingernails against the top of her elongated, podium-style desk.

She picks up a clipboard and skims over the list of names. "Oh right, B-E-L-L-E. Here you are. Sign in, right next to your name, please. You're slotted for 9:53 a.m." She smiles as she hands me the clipboard along with an ink pen. "I'm Liza, by the way."

"It's great to meet you, Liza."

She focuses on me with her head cocked and her perfectly shaped eyebrows furrowed as I hand her the clipboard. "You look like you've had a rough start to your day. How about I loan you something to put over your dress? You know, to cover up that stain?"

"You'd do that for me?"

"Absolutely." She removes a beautiful hot-pink cashmere scarf hanging on the back of her swivel desk chair and hands it to me. "Here you go, sweetie. This should do the trick."

"Oh my! Are you sure it's okay?"

"Girl Scout's Honor. I would be beside myself if I didn't lend a helping hand. Besides, like I was about to mention just before the phone interruption, jelly donuts seem to be a—"

The phone rings again and this time, Liza mouths the words, "I'm so sorry."

I take the free moment to tie the scarf around my neck and let it hang slightly—just enough to cover the drastic stain.

Liza ends the call and informs me it's time for her to escort me to my interview. She places a telephone headset over her ears, maneuvers her way from around her desk, and motions for me to follow.

"This way, hon."

I follow close behind as we enter a hallway, accessible only via her keycard. Liza seems as sweet as she is stylish. She's wearing a cute black-and-white knee-length dress, black high-heeled pumps, and her blond hair is secured in a chic bun. She reminds me of a modern-day pinup girl.

Our walk down the hall comes to a halt as Liza points straight ahead. "Your interview will be right through those double doors. Just let me give you a brief rundown."

I nod, giving her my undivided attention as she leans against the bare wall.

"Okay, so as you know, Antonio Michaels is looking for a new Personal Assistant. He's insisted he conduct the interviews on his own and so far, out of maybe two dozen, he hasn't been the least bit impressed."

She looks at me puzzled, then in an almost motherly fashion, approaches me and pats down a piece of my hair that must look out of place.

"Anyhow," she continues, "just hand Antonio your résumé and let things progress from there. He's looking for some type of connection. Dottie, his last PA, retired last month. She's kind of got big shoes to fill because she had the ability to keep Antonio in line. He's kind of…well, I don't want to share too much more. It may make ya nervous."

"I'm not nervous. After the morning I had on the Metro, I'm feeling like nothing could be worse."

"You rode the Metro here this morning?" She checks her watch.

"Yep. But I got off the train too soon and walked about four blocks."

"You did appear to be a bit flustered when you approached my desk. Come on. You're up."

She leads the way, closer to the double doors, and I must admit, the anticipation of the unknown has surfaced.

What will this Antonio guy be like?

Will he have tough questions for me?

Will he scoff at my lack of PA experience?

We reach the double doors that, incidentally, look a lot larger now than they did ten seconds ago.

Liza smiles. "Funny thing," she says as she slowly turns the knob to open the door, "Antonio also had a jelly-donut-related incident on his way to work this morning. Maybe it's something you can use as an ice breaker? It may help you connect with him."

"Wait. What?" I almost stop in my tracks. "That's an odd coincidence. But a good enough ice breaker if you ask me," I say.

We enter the spacious office and right away, I can't help but notice the bay window that overlooks Downtown Los Angeles. The view is breathtaking—I could seriously get used to working in an office like this.

A tall, dark-haired, slender man in a dark blue suit is facing the large window with his hands securely nestled in the pockets of his perfectly creased slacks.

"Mr. Michaels? Your 9:53 interview is here," Liza says, then looks to me and whispers the words 'good luck' before making a quick exit.

"Just have a seat and I'll be right with you," he says, still facing the window.

I make my way toward one of the high-back chairs in front of what I assume is his desk.

He turns to walk toward the desk and our eyes lock. The look on his face is probably the same look fixed on my own—a look of unfathomable shock, although his is embellished with an impish grin.

"Well, well, well. If it isn't Miss Potty Mouth herself. *You're* my 9:53 interview?" says *Antonio Michaels*...formally known as the jelly-donut-eating, rude guy from the Metro.

And uh...someone better call in the cavalry; the bad day snowball has officially reached monumental avalanche status.

CHAPTER 2

ANTONIO

"Y ou've got to be kidding me," grumbles the fiery woman I encountered earlier this morning on the Metro.

Truthfully, I hardly expected to see her again. Especially since I *never* take the Metro or any other form of public transportation. However, as part of our annual wager-fest, my buddy Jonah bet me a thousand bucks and a round of drinks that I'd never step foot on any form of Los Angeles public transportation.

So, for the first time—ever—I hastily embarked on a public transportation venture. I don't need the one-thousand dollars I'm set to earn from this wager. But I have yet to lose an annual bet. I simply hate losing…at anything.

Of course, Jonah was more than obliged to drop me off at the Metro station, saying he wanted to be sure I actually got on the train, making jokes as soon as I sat in his car.

"Dude," he began, "part of me wants to get on the train with you, hit record, and spread that shit all over YouTube, Snapchat, and Facebook. *No* one is gonna believe your prissy-perfecto ass is taking the Metro."

I flipped him the bird then adjusted the passenger seat of

his Tesla to a comfortable reclining position. "Just shut up and drive. I don't wanna miss that train. And you, Sir-Jokes-A-Lot, should get prepared to pay the hell up. I'll take my thousand bucks divided up in crisp one-hundred-dollar bills. Please and thank you," I said with an insolent chuckle.

Jonah was certainly one to talk. He too has never taken public transportation. Being a product of money, he fits the bill of all clichés related to growing up in the 90210—Beverly Hills.

"I'll gladly pay up when the task has been fulfilled. By the way," he lightly punched my shoulder, "when are you gonna tell me what I have to do this year for wager-fest? You're like, way behind on that shit, man."

"I know. I've been busy planning *CraveMe's* contribution to the upcoming Fashion Show and Lingerie Ball. Man, with Dottie retiring, I've got my hands full. I'll think of something soon, even though it won't quite matter. You always lose."

Jonah grimaced at my comment, making me laugh in amusement. Then, I dutifully gave him a shoulder punch in return.

When we arrived at a stoplight, Jonah reached over to the backseat, then tossed me a small white paper bag. "Here you go. I was generous enough to buy you some breakfast."

I opened the bag and took a quick look inside. "Dude, really? Jelly donuts?"

"Fuck yeah. You might as well reward yourself for putting on your big-boy boxers by getting up the nerve to take the train." He let out an exaggerated laugh while covering his mouth with his hand. "I'm really surprised you made it *this* far. Shit, I might even pay you *two* thousand bucks."

"Oh, believe me, you'll pay up. Just be on time when you pick me up at my office later on today with payment in hand," I demanded.

"And will I get to see the beautiful Miss Liza? I'm telling you, that woman is so fucking fierce. I'd convince her to marry me *today* if she'd only talk to me," Jonah said, raising both eyebrows expressively. He's had a thing for my receptionist for the past two years. He just doesn't get that she'll probably never give him the time of day.

"Sorry, dude. Liza's just not that into you."

Jonah barreled into the Metro station like Speed-Racer 2.0, minutes before the train was due to arrive. "Oh, and come to think of it," I announced before closing the door of his shiny new Tesla. "I've got the perfect bet for you. I officially bet you a thousand bucks you'll get *no*where with Liza."

Jonah's jaw dropped and the dumbfounded look of shock that consumed his perfectly round face, was priceless.

By the time I boarded the train and took a seat, my stomach was growling like a ninja wolf. Despite the fact that a jelly donut would be the last thing I would ever indulge in, I reached into the bag, pulled one of those bad boys out, and bit right in. Before I knew it, the train took off. I found myself taking in the scenery, fascinatingly immersed in everyone around me. There were riders of all types: students, businessmen and women, a mixture of those who appeared to be homeless, touristy types, and those who looked like they just took the Metro to pass the time.

About twenty minutes later, the train came to a grinding halt, and as some jumped off, others hopped on. At this point in my train-riding endeavor, it was standing room only, and I graciously gave up my seat to a little elderly lady who was hauling groceries. She reminded me of my grandma back in Italy.

So anyway, I digress…

I moved toward the back of the train and parked myself up against a pole for support. I reached into the paper bag, removed the second donut, and took a hefty bite.

And *that's* when I saw her.

She appeared to be deep in thought, one hand clenched to the strap of her oversized designer bag, while the other hand was clenched to her cell phone. She carried herself with this naive, yet classy, allurement—as if she had no clue about her level of drop-dead-gorgeousness.

I tried, but couldn't take my eyes off of her and neither could those she eased past, most of them doing a double-take.

Her shiny black hair, long and straight, seemed to highlight her cappuccino-colored skin tone—a tone that made every revealing inch of her body look as though it had been personally kissed by the sun.

As if that wasn't enough, she wore an off-white sweater dress that tastefully clung to her body, showcasing an hour-glass figure that would make Kim Kardashian's own curves gawk in envious admiration.

And icing on the cake: hot-pink five-inch stilettos that hoisted her petite body to a perfect-for-me height.

I swear, the woman was undoubtedly JDH.

Jaw. Dropping. Hot.

So there I was, all prepared to flash my Colgate smile as she walked by. But instead, as if in slow motion, she tripped on some guy's briefcase and landed up against me and that damn jelly donut.

It was a beyond epic fail moment—for her anyway. All I could manage to spill out of my mouth was the word, *whoops*. I meant no disrespect as I continued to eat my way through the rest of the donut—what else was I supposed to do? I had to get rid of it, right?

Her reaction was downright unexpected, catching me completely off-guard.

Why?

Because instead of thanking me and treating me like a hero for saving her from falling flat on her face, she scolded me.

That's right, she scolded *me*…Antonio Michaels.

And I found it annoyingly…sexy.

Sure, I probably could've been a tad sympathetic about

how the red jelly from my donut left an extremely noticeable mark on the top half of her dress. But truth be told, the woman made me nervous.

No woman makes me nervous.

Anyway, she glared at me with those big green, cat-shaped eyes, and I almost melted. And don't let me begin to describe how good the woman smelled.

Yet, she proved to be quite a spicy little dish—armed with an attitude and a mouth that spit out cuss words as nonchalantly as a back-in-the-day baseball player spit out chewing tobacco.

Despite all of that, the potty-mouthed kryptonite-like woman has been renting the overly-crowded space in my mind ever since our encounter on the train. And now, like some unbelievably bizarre twist of fate, she's standing here.

In my office.

Looking even hotter than I remembered.

"*You're* Antonio Michaels?" She shakes her head and rolls her eyes, seeming to look a little disgusted.

I take slow, *I'm a cool guy* strides toward my desk, trying to shield how delighted I am to see her. "Yep. Last time I checked."

Don't be a dick. I internally remind myself.

She scoffs. "Of course you are. Look, I'm gonna save you the trouble and leave. Obviously, our impromptu meeting earlier would suggest we're *not* at all what one would consider to be working relationship material."

I see she's still armed with that saucy *bite me* coating.

With a sultry swing of her hair and one hand on her hip, she pivots and stomps out of my office.

Instinctively, I rush after her, but, like an idiot, I stumble over one of my oversized desk chairs. "Wait!" I call out; yet, like a swift flash of lightning, she darts completely out of sight.

By the time I reach Liza at the front receptionist desk, Miss Potty Mouth is nowhere to be seen.

Damn it.

"Antonio, is everything okay?" Liza asks, rising up from the seat behind her desk.

"Do you happen to know the name of my 9:53 interview?" I ask, hoping Liza has some sort of information.

"Oh, you mean the woman who darted out of here as if she saw a ghost? Um, what just happened?"

"Her name, Liza. What's her name?" I walk over to her desk, raking all ten of my fingers through my hair—something I tend to do when I'm earnestly focused on a project.

"Belle with an E. Her name is Daniella Belle. Didn't she give you her résumé?"

I shake my head. "Nope. We didn't even make it that far into the interview. But I want—scratch that—I *need* her to be my personal assistant." I straighten my suit jacket and turn to head toward the doorway that leads to my office. "Find her please, Liza. Just find her," I direct, swiping my keycard to open the door.

"Okay. I'll certainly try my best. She does have my scarf, after all. Oh, and, Antonio?" Liza says, her voice timid.

"Yes, Liza?" I pivot to face her as I hold the door open.

"Just so you know, TMZ is reporting that you were on the Metro this morning and had a heated confrontation with another passenger. Something about a viral video they plan to post on their show this afternoon. Shall I forward this to Public Relations? I'm sure they've got you mixed up with someone else." She shrugs and smirks. "Like you'd ever take the train to work, right?"

CHAPTER 3

DANIELLA

"Holy shit, D! You're a total celeb now," Emma announces as she unreservedly charges into my bedroom.

"Language. Watch your language young lady," I nag, wondering what the hell she's so wound-up about.

Emma can be quite the drama queen, as is the case with most sixteen-year-old girls. Come to think of it, I've known her to be prone to dramatic tendencies since I became her nanny five years ago.

"My language? Ha! You should talk." She giggles, peering down at the tablet she's holding. "At least I didn't get called a potty mouth in front of a gazillion people."

Emma plops down beside me on my bed, seeming to ignore the practically infinite amount of candy bar wrappers that are scattered about.

Ever since I returned home from that ill-fated train ride and equally ill-fated job interview, I've been dolefully feasting on a substantial assortment of junk food while binge-watching *Pretty Little Liars*. To think how promptly my day morphed into a Mt.-Everest-sized heap of crap. I mean, honestly: from that bitchy break up text, to a less-than-to-be-desired occurrence with the Rude Hottie Guy on the Metro, to an it's-never-gonna-happen-job interview with said Rude Hottie Guy—without a single measure of doubt, today will go down in the history of *what-the-fuck?* days.

By the time I got home, I wanted nothing more than to indulge in a pity-party-junk-food-fest in my bedroom, taking full advantage of Emma being at school and Stacy being at work.

However, now Emma is home from school…calling for me to put on my 'nanny hat' as her big brown eyes switch from gleaming up at me, to being engrossed in whatever the heck she finds so intriguing on her tablet.

Aiming the remote control toward the TV, I push the button to pause *Pretty Little Liars* and turn over to face Emma. "What on Earth are you talking about?"

Emma peers up at me with utter amusement darting from her eyes. She passes her tablet over to me. "Here. Take a look at what's trending all over TMZ's YouTube Channel right now."

I grab the tablet, fully expecting something related to some band she's into. Instead, it's a video with the tagline: *Bombshell Brunette "Miss Potty Mouth" and* CraveMe *CEO, Antonio Michaels, Have A Feudal Exchange On The Los Angeles Metro.*

Holy. Hell.

No…

Emma lets out an ear-piercing squeal as she reaches over to tap the play button on the video. "I wanna watch it again," she says. "It's quite hilarious."

I can feel my heart pounding in painstaking anticipation.

This truly *cannot* be happening.

Seriously…

A video?

A *viral* video.

Apparently, the daft *streamer* captured the whole-entire-incident—at least from the moment I can be seen and heard telling Antonio Michaels exactly what he was expertly portraying: A First-Class Jerk. And, of course, the now-viral video, that has over two-million views, ends with the High and Mighty Antonio Michaels referring to me as...Miss Potty Mouth.

Emma cocks her head to the side, and even though I turn my head to shamefully avoid eye contact, I can literally feel her laser-beamed judgmental gaze upon me. "Miss Potty Mouth?" She laughs. "You must admit, D, this video is superbly epic."

"Oh, you're right. It is indeed epic. An epic fail," I say, beginning to feel queasy from all of the junk food consumed. Or queasy from the viral video, perhaps. "And stop calling me D," I demand, attempting to surreptitiously change the subject.

"Fine. Shall I call you Miss Potty Mouth instead?" Emma laughs, and I pick up a pillow then playfully smack her across the head with it.

"You've gotta spill the details, D."

"Believe me, Emma. There's really nothing to spill. I had it out on the train this morning with another commuter. The guy just so happened to be the CEO with whom I had a scheduled interview." I cover my face with a pillow and mumble, "So, you know, just another day in the life of Daniella Belle."

Emma removes the pillow off of my face and her frivolous gaze meets my solemn one. "D...it was Antonio *he's so hot* Michaels. So, you're a total fifteen-minute celeb now."

"A fifteen-minute celeb?" I look at Emma, feeling a little dazed.

"You know...fifteen minutes of fame? Duh."

I roll my eyes. "Oh. Right. Duh."

Emma glances at the digital clock on my bedside table, then reaches for the remote control to my TV. "It's 2.59.

TMZ comes on at 3. Your *incident* is bound to be their top story."

With the remote in hand, Emma un-pauses *Pretty Little Liars* and scrolls down the channel program guide to TMZ. Sure enough, their lead story is me and Antonio Michaels on the Metro.

Great. What's next? I'll get struck by lightning?

Like a groupie, Emma becomes fixated on the popular gossip TV show, now reporting on me as the mystery bombshell potty mouth. I turn over on my side, pulling the cover up and over my head as if the thin sheet is enough to shield my trivial embarrassment.

All I wanted was a chance at a job with a well-known lingerie company, in hopes that someday I'd be able to share and implement the designs of my very own lingerie line.

But that opportunity has been neglectfully thrust out the window, now lavishly flowing in the wind, off to who-the-fuck-knows-or-even-cares-where land.

I'll get over it. I always do.

Emma squeals, shakes the side of my hip, and yanks the cover from off my head. "Look, D! A live TMZ crew has caught up with Antonio. Just look at him. He's so yummy!"

I turn to watch the TV and just like Emma squealed about, TMZ seems to be following Antonio Michaels as he exits his office building.

And yes. Admittedly he is looking *absolutely* yummy.

But he's still a jerk. A yummy jerk.

Emma turns up the volume, and I can't help but sit up, now becoming fully hooked on what's unfolding.

"Mr. Michaels!" a TMZ reporter calls out.

The camera swiftly zooms in on the reporter as he gallops toward the lingerie empire CEO.

Acting as though rightfully determined, the popular TMZ reporter shoves a microphone in Antonio's face. "Please tell us what you know about the woman on the train. Is she some sort of acquaintance of yours? A scorned ex-girlfriend, perhaps?"

Antonio snickers as his lips curve into a sportive grin. "All I can say is, I too am fervently trying to find the mystery woman, so if you guys happen to bump into her, please feel free to let me know." He chuckles and appears to look directly into the lens of the camera. Producing what is unarguably a flirtatious gleam, he candidly blasts to all TV viewers, "Miss Potty Mouth? If you happen to be watching this, I'd still like to continue with that interview. Seems as though you could very well be just what I've been searching for—a no-holds-barred fireball."

And just as I forecasted...

There goes that lightning strike.

CHAPTER 4

ANTONIO

ustom-rimmed tires on Jonah's Tesla scream as he erratically peels out of the parking lot of my downtown office. "TM-*fucking*-Z, man? Really?"

"I know, right? You see what happens when I decide to ride the Metro?"

I sway side to side, my fingers gripping the car's interior handle while Jonah mimics *The Fast and The Furious*, dashing in and out of traffic—trying to evade the zealous TMZ paparazzi. He peers through the rearview mirror as he turns the corner, plowing into a cramped alley.

He rolls past a homeless man pushing a shopping cart full of *accouterments* before jolting to a halt in front of a trash dumpster.

"There." He exhales. "I think I may have lost them." Jonah turns to face me, hazel eyes narrowed, glaring at me as if he were a coach about to chew out the star quarterback. "Now where to, Your Freakin' Majesty?"

I hate when he calls me that. As if I'm Prince Charming and he's my very own equerry. I should be so lucky.

"My house. And can you turn off Duran Duran—play

something much more *now*? I guess you probably don't realize we're not living in the 1980s."

Admittedly, Jonah is a pretty cool guy, despite his obsession with the 1980s. Depeche Mode. Duran Duran. The Cure. *Everything* '80s. Including his wardrobe. Blazer. T-shirt. Jeans. He looks like Rico Tubbs straight out of that '80s cop show, *Miami Vice.*

He cranks up the volume, loud enough to irritate me. "Dude. The '80s was *the shit*. Don't knock music from my era." He moves his head to the music.

"Man"—I shoot him an over-exaggerated eye-roll —"you're not even from the '80s. You were born in the '90s."

"Barely. I was meant to be an '80s kid. If only I'd been born a minute earlier, I would have at least made 1989."

It's annoyingly true. Jonah was born January 1st, 1990 at 12 a.m. He's been late to everything ever since.

He pulls out of the alley and, minutes later, we're on the busy freeway, making our way toward my home in Beverly Hills.

"Why is it that every time you end up on TMZ, it's behind a chick?"

He's got a valid point. But the last time it was because a scorned ex-girlfriend rented billboard space featuring my home address. She also claimed to have sold details of my personal life to some tabloids. The woman teetered a little on the cray-cray side. Tinder. I should have swiped left.

"Yeah well, you know I haven't had the best of luck with women. It's hard to find someone interested in just *me*." I reach into my jacket pocket and pull out my phone to check email messages.

"Are you getting nervous, man?" he asks with a slight grin.

I toss him a guarded look. "Nervous about what?"

"Oh, you know what," he says, one thick eyebrow lifted,

hands firmly attached to the steering wheel, as he darts into the carpool lane.

"I try hard not to think or talk about it. So, if you don't mind—"

"Antonio." He breaks into my attempt at an allusive response. "You can't keep putting it off. I mean, if I were you I'd be shitting mega-sized bricks right about now."

But he's not me.

"Look." I shove my phone back into my pocket. "I do appreciate your concern. But honestly man, this is my problem, not yours. I'll figure it all out."

I hope.

Jonah rolls his shoulder, then raises a mocking thumbs-up. "Right. But I'd hate to be the one to say, 'I told you so'."

I shift my gaze to peer out the tinted window as we zoom past cars on the freeway.

Like a fuckin' broken record, Jonah's words play in my head over and over and over again: *Are you nervous? You can't keep putting it off.*

If only I could put off my 30th birthday. Normally, it wouldn't be an issue. But for me, being single on my 30th birthday could be viewed by some as a potential lifestyle changer.

"I'll focus on that crap, just as soon as the Fashion Show and Lingerie Ball are done and over with." I look back at Jonah who has cranked up the six-speaker stereo, this time bobbing his head to music of The Cure.

I should have caught an Uber.

"I'm already packed." He looks at me, his smile as mischievous as the Joker's.

Of course he's already packed. The Fashion Show is all he talks about.

Every. Single. Year.

It's an annual affair in Milan, Italy that *CraveMe* has never missed. Naturally, Jonah attends the event each year since *CraveMe* is one of his Marketing Firm's top clients. He's good at video editing and always seems to capture flawless images of the Fashion Show. He then transforms them into trendsetting brand promos.

I let out a soft chuckle. "Why am I not at all surprised you're already packed?"

With a lopsided smirk Jonah looks at me. "You know I can't disappoint the beautiful ladies of Milan. I packed all my *GQ man of the year* shit. I'm leaving Milan with a girlfriend this year. You watch."

That would be Jonah's ceremonial proclamation. Truth is, he's been searching for a girlfriend now for the past four years. But no woman can seem to measure up to whatever embellished expectation he has.

Exiting the freeway, he drives along Wilshire Blvd, eventually turning onto Beverly Drive.

"Thanks for picking me up and losing TMZ, man. I've had enough viral videos and flashing cameras for the day."

"No worries, my man. What's up with that chick anyway? Miss Potty Mouth? She certainly is a hottie. I saw the video trending all over the internet. Pretty funny." He pulls up my long driveway then the car rolls to a stop.

I open the door and jump out, patting my pockets, making sure I've got my phone and keys. "Her *name* is Daniella and all I know is, I'm dying to find her. Liza is searching every possible source. She'll text me as soon as she locates her."

Jonah raises two skeptical eyebrows. "Well, alrighty then. Good luck with that. I'll catch you later."

I shut the door, whack the roof of the car, then Jonah speeds off toward his house…which is, incidentally, on the same block.

But don't judge us. The two of us are like the brothers we never had.

SEVERAL HOURS HAVE PASSED AND THE MEDIA IS *STILL* RELENTLESS in their coverage of me. Don't they have more interesting guys to report on?

Surely some Pop-star must be having an onstage concert meltdown somewhere.

The crisp February air skates across my face as I open the glass sliding door and step out into my backyard. The view is sedative. Just what I need. I've lived in this house, this city, this *way*, for my entire life.

I'll admit it's a grandiose lifestyle. But I crave change. Something fresh. Different. Unexpected.

Something—

The sound of my phone's sharp tone thrusts me out of my pensive *I hate being a rich guy* moment.

A text from Liza.

Liza: **Hey Boss. Great news!**

I can feel the corner of my mouth lift into a smile.

Could she have found Daniella?

Oh God, please, yes.

Me: **I can use some great news.**

Liza: **I found Miss Potty Mouth! Seems she's a nanny for an entertainment lawyer in Beverly Hills.**

Me: Wait. So she's a nanny?

Maybe Liza texted the word *nanny* in error.

Autocorrect always fails.

Like the time I texted an investment banker that I was looking forward to riding his kick-ass body when I meant to text I was looking forward to riding his kick-ass boat.

Yeah. That was a definite fail.

Thirty, long seconds later, Liza replies.

Liza: **Yes. A live-in nanny. Anyway, would you like her address?**

I allow the text to simmer in my brain before I respond. I

mean, do I really want to just show up to this woman—Daniella's residence?

Seconds later, thumbs trembling in excitement, I text my reply.

Me: **Hell yeah.**

CHAPTER 5

DANIELLA

S even.

My lucky number.

It's also the age I was when I began sketching, designing, and sewing outfits for my doll babies. Six months later, I ingeniously set up shop in the basement of my foster mom's house and began making, then selling doll clothes to all the little girls on the block. I was making a killing. At least until my two trollish foster sisters squealed. My foster mom went full-on RoboCop, shutting down my operation, as if I were the neighborhood dope dealer.

Memories.

That's what's been sweeping through my mind since I decided to bask in the delight of having the house all to myself for the entire week.

Stacy will be heading to New York for a drab convention and Emma's already left to spend a week with her dad. Even if Emma were here, it's not like she truly *needs* me. Not like she did five years ago, anyway. Being a full-time nanny to a sixteen—almost seventeen-year-old—is nearly non-existent compared to that of an eleven-year-old. Which is why I was so looking forward to getting that Personal Assistant job at *CraveMe*.

In all actuality, finding work anywhere but here is a must. I can't expect to stay, working as a nanny to a *seventeen*-year-old. Don't get me wrong; my living arrangements are pretty spectacular. I've got an eight-hundred-square foot en-suite-style bedroom and full privileges in this exquisite home, not to mention a generous monthly stipend that I've been able to stow away in a savings account for the last five years. Sure, as a nanny, I'm expected to clean, cook, do laundry, run errands, etc. But I'm no damn Cinderella, and the older Emma gets, the more awkward it is to be called her nanny.

My plan was to take on the gig as the PA, move into my own place, and eventually work up the nerve to present my portfolio to whomever is in charge of design submissions.

Yet, since that opportunity got all screwed up, I submitted seven online applications this evening to all sorts of jobs, hoping and dreaming for a break.

Any break.

I pour myself a second glass of Merlot, prance my half-tipsy ass into my bathroom to draw a luxurious bubble-filled bath, and push the play button on my MP3, blasting the hell out of Pat Benitar's *Love is a Battlefield*.

Don't you dare judge me. I mean who doesn't fancy songs from the '80s?

The bubble-filled bath summons me with its tranquilizing lavender scent, sudsy clouds of bliss, and the flickering of lights from neon-colored flameless candles I've placed along the edge of the tub.

I peel off my clothes, twist my hair into an unkempt bun, and descend into my toasty bubble cocoon, with wine glass in hand, finding solitude as I escape from today's lousy events.

Tomorrow will be a better day.

No breakup text message, no Metro train crowds, no jelly

donuts, no TV reports featuring Yours Truly, and absolutely no Antonio Michaels.

IT'S BEEN OVER AN HOUR NOW. THE WATER HAS COOLED, BUBBLES dissipated, wine digested, and my MP3 has completed the bubble-bath playlist. I'm beyond relaxed, feeling the way I do after a massage, a first kiss, or a toe-curling orgasm—the kind I haven't had in ages, by the way.

The house is quiet, the sound of the bathtub faucet's perpetual drip echoing in the placidity.

I squeeze my eyes shut, hypnotized by the sound.

Drip. Drip. Drip—

Ding Dong.

What the fuck?

My eyes spring open at the intrusive, bell-tower-like toll.

The doorbell? Perhaps I heard wrong—drifted off and dreamt of the doorbell ringing?

Ding Dong.

I stiffen, slightly startled by the tone.

It's definitely the doorbell.

Water glides off me as I rise up. Grabbing the oversized towel off the rack, I drape it around me, stepping out of the tub, one foot at a time, onto the plush white rug. I quickly dry myself off, then the towel pools around my ankles as I reach for the black satin robe hanging on the hook by the bathroom door. I slip into the robe and rush to the front door, turning on lights as I race closer.

I can just kill Emma. She always forgets to close the gate when she leaves, practically inviting solicitors to the front door. And it's probably little Sarah from across the street, fixed on selling me another damn box of Girl Scout Cookies. She knows I've got a terrible weakness for Thin Mints.

The bell rings again and I swing the door open, fully prepared to send little Sarah on her way.

No cookies today, Sarah, sorry.

Only, it's *not* Sarah.

Why can't it be Sarah?

I fidget, clenching the front part of my robe with one hand, and pat my unkempt bun with the other.

My cheeks are on fire. *What is he even doing here?*

Antonio *fucking* Michaels.

And, *God*, does he look perfectly amazing.

Leather jacket. Light blue jeans. Black, pectoral-hugging T-shirt. Oxford shoes.

"Hey." A smile dances on his lips as his heady, dark blue eyes give me a sweeping once-over.

"If you're looking for jelly donuts, you'll have to look elsewhere," I say, nose in the air, flashing a cynical side-eye.

He rubs his chin, smirks, and props his hand up against the door frame. "Do you ever have anything nice to say?"

"Probably not." I resist the urge to chuckle, despite the fact my lips have curved their way into a half-smile.

He runs his tongue across his upper lip, and I can see a playful gleam in his eyes as he surveys my ensemble.

Satin robe. Barefoot. Messy hair.

All that's missing to round out my *appearance* is a light green mud mask splattered over my entire face.

"Is this a bad time?" The sarcastic tone darts out of his mouth like a cork bursting out of a champagne bottle.

"I was having a relaxing bath. You know, to forget all about today's events." I glare at him and fold my arms, the realization of him standing at my door just settling in. "And what are you doing here? How did you find me?"

"Yeah. About that." He taps his fingers along the edge of the door frame and briefly looks toward the sky before shifting his gaze back to me. "I was hoping we could go forward with the interview. For the PA position?"

I stare at him for ten long seconds, maybe even more, before shrugging.

"Listen," he says, his shoulder now leaning on the door frame. "I know we had a rough start today, but there's something about you I find—"

"Okay," I interrupt. "When and where would you like to have this interview? Tomorrow? Your downtown office again?"

With raised eyebrows, he replies in an inviting purr-like tone that makes my sensitive lady parts beg for a cold shower. "How about right now?"

CHAPTER 6

DANIELLA

"**W**hat the hell do you mean he just showed up?" Stacy's bark echoes over the loudspeaker of my phone that sits on one of the many shoe shelves in my walk-in closet.

I'm frantically searching for something to wear.

Something impressive. Interview-y.

"I don't know. Just like that—*poof*—he magically appeared and now he's in the living room waiting to take me to *Fornaio*." I toss another unworthy article of clothing onto the closet floor. "Believe me, I'm just as shocked as you are."

"So, he wants to conduct an interview? Right now? As in tonight? At *Fornaio*? That's a pretty upscale restaurant for a job interview." Her mockery radiates through the phone. "Does he look as hot as he did on that TMZ interview?"

"Stacy!" I growl. "Now is so not the time to be joking around." I pause, still in my closet, looking at my reflection in the floor-length mirror. "But, yes. Even hotter."

"I knew it." She lets out a victory laugh. "What are you gonna wear?"

I shrug even though she can't see me and continue my

frantic search. "Maybe I'll just go dressed as I am right now. Black lacy bra. Black—just as lacy—panties. Black stilettos."

"You're so damn cute when you're being sarcastic. Anyway, you know I'm no fashion guru, but I do think your black pencil skirt and that beige cashmere sweater Emma got you for Christmas will look smashing. Actually, whatever you wear will be fine."

"Then bra, panties, and stilettos it is," I kid.

"Well, let me know how it goes, love. Just text me. I'll be on that flight to New York by the time you get back home, no doubt."

"Sounds good. Have a safe flight."

"Thanks, babe. And good luck."

After yanking the beige cashmere sweater and pencil skirt off of their hangers, I slip them on and survey my getup in the mirror.

Elle Woods meets Charlotte York.

Totally works for me.

I work my hair into a wispy ponytail, apply a few light coats of mascara, and give my lips a dab of light pink lip gloss, then grab my handbag, résumé, and letter of recommendation. Blowing this second-chance interview would be a travesty. Sure, Antonio is still a yummy jerk, yet the opportunity to work for him is undoubtedly the break I need. And even though him showing up here is oddly unconventional, I look at this as another chance to make a great impression.

My heart thumps harder as I turn the corner out of the hallway and into the living room.

I take in a deep, calming breath.

It doesn't help.

The sight of Antonio—Tall strapping, Christian Grey 2.0—makes my stomach do triple, Olympian-style back flips.

I walk toward him and the sound of my high heels tapping the hard tile floor seems to abruptly divert his attention from the screen of his phone—to me.

His mouth drops as he rises from his comfortable sitting position on the light blue patterned accent chair. "You look... lovely. And I uh, promise not to get any food on your clothes this evening."

His wry smile produces an alluring dimple.

So. Fucking. Sexy.

And definitely something I hadn't noticed on the Metro.

But I know men like him.

Mesmeric. Flirty. Womanizing.

Through copious Google research, I learned Antonio Michaels has a thing for models. In fact, articles showcase him with a new model wrapped in his arms every single month. Everyone knows the Internet doesn't lie.

So, I won't allow myself to become distracted by his... sultry glory.

Thankfully, I've sworn off men—and I'm gonna stick to that safety mantra like honey sap on a tree.

CHAPTER 7

ANTONIO

C uss words generally aren't my thing…but, holy *fuck*, she's hot.

Maybe this is a bad idea. Clearly, I'm far more suited to have an Ugly Betty type of a Personal Assistant.

Not Goddess Daniella.

"What?" she says as if she can read my thoughts.

But, thank God, she can't.

"What…what?" I respond—a dismal attempt at being sly. I look away for a minute and push the start button of my car, trying to appear un-captivated. Then my gaze gravitates right back toward her.

She fastens her seat belt and delicately parts her lips. "You had a strange expression on your face."

"I was merely waiting for you to fasten your seat belt," I lie. "You know…safety first."

Seductive, cat-shaped eyes glare at me. "Right."

She smells of flowers, lavender, and butterscotch candy. The same bewitching scent I impulsively inhaled when she was standing next to me this morning on the Metro. I'm starting to believe I just might be in some serious trouble here.

While cruising along Sunset Blvd, the atmosphere

between the two of us is stoic. I'm sure, like me, Daniella's paralyzed by her own thoughts of how this interview will turn out.

"Is this your car?" she asks, abruptly breaking the silence.

"Yes. Why wouldn't it be?"

"Well, we did collide on the Metro this morning."

"Yeah," I run my fingers through my hair, "that was based on a bet."

She shifts in her seat, now facing me with her arms folded. "A bet?" She lifts a brow.

I let out a subtle chuckle. "Yep. Something called wager-fest. My buddy and I do it every year. This year he bet me I would never ride the Metro. So I did. This morning. And of course, I won the wager."

Daniella nods. "I see. So our bumping into each other, in *that* manner, was completely fortuitous."

"May not have happened any other way."

"Maybe so. But it would have been far more worthwhile if you weren't eating that donut."

"Or if you weren't texting and walking. They issue tickets for that sort of thing now." I laugh.

She giggles and it's the first time I've seen her flash a smile.

And it's utterly breathtaking.

As soon as I pull to a stop in front of *Fornaio*, a red-vested valet rushes to open the passenger door. He helps Daniella out, and she stands alongside the curb, twirling a strand of her long ebony locks around her finger as she waits for me to join her.

She looks nervous now, which selfishly puts me a little more at ease.

"I've never been here," she reports in a stern voice, now fidgeting with a large envelope.

"What's in there?"

"Oh." She looks at the envelope she holds firmly against her chest. "My résumé."

"Oh, yes." I nod. "Of course."

Duh. This is a job interview, I remind myself.

Inside, Domenico, the waiter, seats the two of us at a table toward the far end of the restaurant. I called ahead, requesting a table away from the crowd so Daniella and I can have a decent conversation without distractions.

"This is one of my favorite restaurants."

She glances up from the menu. "Excellent. Then you shouldn't have a problem recommending something."

She's perfectly sassy.

I cock my head. "Depends on what you're in the mood for."

She smirks, tucking a loose strand of hair behind her ear. "Something superbly fattening. It's been a most tedious day."

"Pizza?" I raise a skeptical eyebrow.

"With everything."

A woman after my own heart.

Domenico drops off two glasses of water and pats me on the back. "Antonio, *amico mio,* it's so wonderful to see you here today," he says, his Italian accent fading after all his years in America. His parents own the restaurant.

"It's good to be here, Domenico…how's the family?"

He steals a quick glance at Daniella, who seems impressed I'm known by name. "Uh, they are just fine. Can I bring you the Italian soda you love so much…and one for your uh— friend?" He looks at Daniella again, and smiles.

"Sure, that sounds fine. And we'll have a pie with everything." I wink at Daniella.

"Of course. I'll return shortly with your sodas and pizza pie, *amico mio,*" he says before making his way to the kitchen.

"Nice to get the VIP treatment. Do you get that everywhere?" she asks, with little effort in masking her sarcastic tone.

"Everywhere but the Metro," I fire back, fighting the urge to flirt. "So, Daniella. Tell me about yourself."

Her eyes quickly narrow—a sure sign I'm about to get scolded again.

"I'm sure you know plenty about me, Mr. Michaels. I would expect nothing less from a man who showed up at my doorstep. So, why don't you tell me what you know, and I'll fill in whatever you haven't uncovered?"

I allow a pause to dance between the two of us as I think of a worthy reply.

"How about you indulge me," I mutter, my fingertips gently tapping the rim of my water glass. "Pretend I know nothing about you." I feel a smirk take over my mouth and give myself a mental high-five for delivering such a smooth rebound.

"Fine," she says, raising her chin as she surrenders to defeat. "Just promise me one thing?"

Uh-oh. This oughta be interesting.

"What's that?"

"Promise me you'll give me a chance. Even if you discover I'm not as qualified as other candidates, I possess something they may not."

I slip her my most curious glance. "And...what's that?"

Besides the ability to make me gawk at you as if you're the only woman in my world.

Settle down, I tell myself.

She takes in a deep breath. "I have an organic passion for all things lingerie. So, in me, not only will you gain an efficiently loyal Personal Assistant, you'll also gain someone who appreciates the significance of lingerie and its influential effect on someone's life."

My jaw drops as I sit across from her, digesting what I deem to be the most culminating *why you should hire me* pitch —ever. I'd be a fool if I didn't give her a chance—little does she realize the job is already hers.

But, for the sake of me carrying on with this…interview, I mustn't give in so casually.

"And in your opinion"—I clear my throat—"just how does lingerie influence someone's life?"

She tugs at her diamond-studded earlobe and squares her shoulders. "Lingerie is more than simple fabric we classify as an undergarment. Lingerie is a woman's alter ego."

Damn, that's actually good. So much so, I may consider using it as a new tagline. *CraveMe Lingerie—A Woman's Alter Ego.*

Domenico delivers a round pan of pizza and props it up between Daniella and me on the table. "*Buon appetito*," he says, placing our Italian sodas down before disappearing to the kitchen.

"Ladies first. Dig in," I command.

She hesitates at first, then leans in, lifts a hefty slice, and takes a bite. "Mmmm," she says with a gratifying eye-roll.

"Best pizza in the 90210," I say, grabbing a slice of my own.

We eat in silence at first, as I study the way she savors each bite of pizza, peeling off pepperoni slices, entrancingly cramming them into her mouth, one by one.

Then I dive straight back into interview mode—before my mind surges off into more slinky contemplation.

"So, suppose I do decide to hire you. How will that affect your life as a nanny?"

Her eyes flicker with perplexity. "You *have* done your research. That's good. And regarding Emma—she's almost seventeen. She doesn't need a nanny. I'm more like her older sister at this point. Stacy, my boss—Emma's mom—is rooting for me to get this job. She gave me a letter of recommenda-tion." Daniella reaches for the envelope that's now nestled underneath a pile of napkins. "Would you like to see it?"

I shake my head. "There are a few things I need to point out about the position, and if afterward you feel you're up for what being my PA entails, then I'll move on to reviewing your résumé and cover letter."

She lifts her brows, looking semi-amused. "Fair enough. Do tell all about what being your PA entails."

Domenico interrupts, by removing the now empty pizza pan and offering dessert.

We both readily decline as we sit across from one another, both serving the other scrutinizing eyes.

Daniella folds her arms, clearly waiting for me to enlighten her.

I lean back a little more comfortably in my chair. "You'll be expected to be on call, available via phone—mostly text—in the event I need to get a hold of you outside of regular office hours. You'll need to attend all meetings with me, taking copious notes, then summarizing them in a follow-up email. You'll arrange all travel, meetings with clients, and converse with vendors and accountants, on my behalf when I'm not available." I pause to allow her a few seconds to digest what's been said. "And of course, there's the ever-so-exclusive Fashion Show and Lingerie Ball. In Milan. You'll be expected to attend," I finally add.

"Milan? As in…Italy?" Her eyes gleam.

I nod. "Yep. In two weeks. It's an annual event. *CraveMe* is usually well-represented." I lower my head, drifting into panic mode as the realization settles in. *Two weeks.* And I'm not the least bit prepared. Dottie always took care of planning what *CraveMe* does each year at the events. But with her gone and my birthday coming up, I've been unable to focus on putting anything together.

"And by *usually*…you mean—"

"Dottie—my last PA—usually took care of it all. And she's not here so I've…fallen a little behind."

She slurps up the last bit of her soda then slightly tilts her head. "For the last five years, I've planned and organized every detail of my boss's life, been on-call twenty-four hours, seven days a week, and have planned all of Emma's parties—from holiday to her Sweet Sixteen—albeit I'll admit none of those are as grandiose as I imagine the Fashion Show and Lingerie Ball to be, but still. The point is, Antonio"—she sits taller in her seat—"I'm your girl. And even though I can almost guarantee I'll screw up now and then, through trial and error, I will eventually become your new and improved Dottie."

I stroke my stubble-laced chin and lean in closer to her side of the table. "You're hired, Miss Daniella Belle. And for the record, you had me with your tenacious snark. You are indeed, my girl."

CHAPTER 8

DANIELLA

I'm frozen.

Completely unable to step foot into *CraveMe's* downtown headquarters.

Nervous? Fuck yeah.

Heart racing.

Sweat glistening along my forehead.

Clumsy.

Okay, well, *clumsy* is just me on a normal day.

But think about it…just yesterday I was a live-in nanny—cooking, cleaning, washing clothes, and running errands.

Now, I'm officially the Personal Assistant to Antonio Michaels.

Stacy seemed giddy when I shared the news via text after I got back home last night—probably even a tad more excited than myself. She said I'm not to worry about leaving her house anytime soon. I still have a place to live, full house privileges and all.

Before going to bed, I ransacked my closet in search of suitable *PA* attire. Appearance equals confidence, and believe me, a potent dose of confidence is needed to boost my esteem.

This morning, I ultimately settled on a smart-looking

pinstripe pant suit and my favorite pair of red, strappy high heels—I love heels just as much as I do lingerie. The two components belong together, like cocoa-dusted whipped cream and a fancy cappuccino.

"Are you gonna just stand there...or are you planning to eventually go in?" Antonio's soft hum buzzes in my ear and I instinctively jump. The word "fuck," escapes my lips, and when I whirl around to face him, he lets out a chuckle.

"The return of Miss Potty Mouth?" He playfully arches both brows. "Or perhaps it's just when you're around me?"

I shift, placing a hand on my hip. "Seems as though you have a subtle way of bringing out the potty mouth in me." I lift my chin in defense and catch a hint of a smile tugging at his lips.

"Hmm. I see." His shoulder grazes mine as he reaches to open the door to the office. "Opening the door is the first step. Now that I've done that for you, please, be my guest and step foot into your new role as Miss Personal Assistant."

He steps over to the door and, while holding it open, waves his hand, motioning me to walk in.

Sauntering past him, I get a generous whiff of his cologne.

Soapy. Musky. Masculine.

With a mild hint of arrogance.

But he's undoubtedly hot.

No wonder women flock to him. That is, at least according to what I've read about him on the Internet.

"Normally, I'd introduce you to the office team. But today's Wednesday," he says, gesturing for me to follow.

He swipes a key card, unlocking the door that opens up to the long hallway leading up to his office. The same office I stormed out of yesterday, like a spoiled diva. I laugh internally at the thought of how I must have looked to him.

"What's the deal with Wednesday?" I say as we reach his office doors.

"Most of my team works from home on Wednesdays.

Including myself. But I forgot all about that last night when I dropped you off at your house." He opens the door. "Have a seat. I'll gather your new-hire paperwork then show you to your office."

I walk over, ease down onto one of the high-back velvet-lined chairs in front of his desk, and cross my legs. "So, it's just the two of us here this morning?"

He sits across from me, a large mahogany desk between us. "No. Hector, our IT guy is here. He opens up the office each day around seven. But he's a like a hermit. You can meet him another day."

I nod as my eyes survey the room.

Gray walls accented by white crown molding.

Walls with framed posters of lingerie-wearing models on the catwalk.

A sleek leather couch that faces floor-to-ceiling windows with panoramic views of the city.

And a desk with two computers, a few file folders, and a small gold-framed photo of a dark-haired woman wearing a flowery dress. The chic black-and-white photo captures the woman smiling as she looks down, her hand caressing her remarkably round belly.

His sister? His *wife*? What if the Internet is wrong? Maybe he's a happily married man with a baby on the way.

The sound of Antonio clearing his throat, interrupts my theorization. "Here's a few papers for you to fill out. Just some information that Liza will enter in the computer tomorrow. You know…your full name, address, emergency contact, etcetera." He hands me the small stack of papers. "You can take them home and bring them back tomorrow, all filled out."

He rises from his chair and straightens the collar on his shirt. "Let me show you to your office."

My office, an extension of his, is quaint and tidy. I snap a quick selfie of me sitting behind my desk and send it to Stacy and Emma, showcasing my elation.

They both immediately reply with a happy face emoji.

Antonio peers in, leaning on the frame of my office door.

Why, oh why, does he have to look so yummy?

Pressed pants. Crisp white button down. Leather shoes.

He's like a goddamn living, breathing front cover of a GQ magazine.

"So, what do you think of your office?" he says, now stepping in.

"It's perfect." I pause as I survey the room. "I'll add some feminine touches to liven it up but, all in all, it's quite fantastic."

He sits down on the edge of my desk, his blue eyes, dark and smoky, momentarily fixed on mine. "Come." He smiles and with his hand, gestures for me to follow. "I have to be in Westwood in an hour for a brainstorming meeting with our marketing firm. You'll need to meet them anyway, so you might as well join me. You can take notes."

"Of course." I stand, collect my purse, along with the stack of new hire paperwork, and follow close behind my new boss, all too eager to begin my first assignment as his personal assistant.

Nervous? Not anymore.

Somehow, I get the rather astute impression I'm going to like it here.

CHAPTER 9

ANTONIO

J onah's eyes widen in absolute amusement the second he sees me strut into the expansive boardroom of Creative Solutions, Inc with Daniella by my side. I'm certain he recognizes her from the video TMZ showcased yesterday.

"My man, my man, my man," he says, coming in strong for a man-hug. "I'm all ready to brainstorm themes for the The Fashion Show. I can't believe it's only weeks away." He gives Daniella a congenial once-over and extends his hand to shake hers. "Hey there. I'm Jonah. You must be Daniella. Antonio's new PA? I've heard loads about you."

I launch a critical glare at him. Fact is, he's right. I haven't stopped talking about Daniella since I laid eyes on her. But she doesn't need to know that.

"All good things, I hope?" Daniella says with a grin.

She looks ravishing today, with a curve-hugging pant suit, sexy heels, and ribbons of her long hair streaming down her back. The two of us chit-chatted during the drive here, and I was able to unveil fragments of key information: she's six years younger than I am, is from Texas, and is newly single, thanks to some idiot who broke up with her yesterday, via text. Coward.

"Yep. All good things. Anyway, shall we begin?" Jonah looks at me with raised eyebrows. "We've got lots to accomplish in such little time."

☉☈☋

TIME FLIES AS JONAH AND I BRAINSTORM FOR OVER AN HOUR. I've found it difficult to concentrate with Daniella seated next to me—feeling as though I'm trapped in some sappy romantic comedy about a hunky guy drooling over a hot chick who won't give him the time of day.

Maybe that's what I find so annoyingly alluring about her: she doesn't seem to give a damn.

"Hello? Earth to Antonio." Jonah's sharp tone cuts into my thoughts.

"Uh…sorry. What?" I grumble, tapping my pen on the tabletop.

"I said, what about an east meets west theme?" He looks as though he believes he's struck gold.

But he hasn't.

"Hell no," I say unquestionably.

"Well, I'm all out of ideas then." He tosses his pen onto his notepad and runs his fingers through his dark, curly hair. "You've turned down a beach theme, a mermaid theme, a bad girl theme, and now this. Need I remind you again we are only weeks away? *Weeks*, Antonio."

Jonah's ideas have been good. Just not good enough. *CraveMe* has been falling behind competitors at The Fashion Show, and I need this year's theme to be freakin' spectacular.

"Look, Jonah," I express, now pacing the black-and-white marble floor of the boardroom. "All of those ideas are great. But I need something different. Something *spectacular*. And definitely something the other guys like *Rendezvous* and other competitors won't be doing." I stop pacing and turn to face Jonah. "*CraveMe* must stand out."

Jonah smirks then looks pointedly at Daniella, who is feverishly scribbling away on the notepad. "What do you think? Have you any ideas?"

I interrupt, throwing my hands in the air. "Hey, now wait. I seriously doubt *she's* even been to The Fashion Show. Besides that, she knows nothing about the brand, being this is her first day and all. I don't think she's remotely qualified to offer any insight."

And just as quickly as the insolent words fly out of my mouth I realize how they must have sounded.

Daniella stiffens and I can see a glimmer of hostility in her eyes as she glares at me.

Through pursed lips she mutters, "With all due respect, Mr. Michaels, perhaps part of the problem is you're quick to dismiss the scope of an idea simply based on your perceived notion. All the themes you've eschewed can be made into something, I believe the word you used was, *spectacular*. You've just got to come down from your higher-than-thou pedestal and give the unknown a chance." The seat scrapes from under her as she shoots up from her chair. She straightens her suit jacket. "If you'll excuse me for a moment, I'd like to visit the powder room."

Jonah and I both follow Daniella with speculative eyes as she marches out of the boardroom.

Jonah's mouth flies open. "Well, isn't she the perfect dose of spunk you've been missing all this time?" He beams and I just want to punch him.

"I deserved it. I insulted her without meaning to. But, as seems her norm, she fired right back."

"You do know she's right? You can't afford to be Arrogant Antonio right now. We've got a fashion show to put on and frankly we've got nothin'."

I sit back down, lowering my head into my hands. "You're right. Time is of the essence. I'll try to keep an open mind and I'll ask Daniella—"

"You'll ask me what?" Daniella queries, as she walks past my seat and slides into hers, seemingly careful not to make eye contact with me.

"If you've got any ideas," I offer, my voice low. "And I apologize for my rant. I'll try to be less of a dick from now on. It's something I'm working on."

"Diligently, I hope?"

I flash a wry smile, and internally scoff at how relentless she is. She's getting to me, in more ways than one.

"Okay, you two. Back to the task at hand," Jonah says, walking over to a flip chart to make notes. He picks up a green marker and points it to Daniella. "Spill it. Your ideas."

Her cheeks brighten as she bites on the tip of her pen. "Well, as Antonio so blatantly pointed out, I've never been to The Fashion Show in Milan." She flashes me a side glance and scoots forward in her chair. "But I do know a tiny bit about fashion shows. I did, after all, work with the renowned Lauren Blake, during Fashion Week in New York, a few years ago, while in design school."

Wait…what? I thought she was just a nanny.

Jonah bites on his balled fist, his eyes animated. "Lauren Blake? She's like a fucking fashion diva. And you worked with her? Props to you, my lady."

Daniella nods. "Right. Anyway, I'd be happy—actually, honored—to share some ideas. But," she looks at me sternly, "seeing as how I know nothing about the brand," she shifts a more amiable glare back to Jonah, "I'll need information. Footage from past events, a catalog filled with *CraveMe* designs, and the amount of time they've allotted for us at this fashion show—"

"We won the bid for thirty minutes on the runway," I proudly interject.

"Congratulations. That's an impressive amount of time." She sets her pen down onto the table and folds her arms. "So, gentlemen, I'll be able to have concrete ideas for you tomorrow morning. Provided I'm given the items mentioned." She faces me again, this time armed with one raised eyebrow and a smug half-grin. "And just so you know, I do own several pieces of *CraveMe* lingerie. In fact, I'm wearing some right now."

Smoldering green eyes stay fixed on mine as if she's waiting to see what affect her comment does to me.

And although I'm burning up inside, imagining how her body looks and feels cradled in some of my sultry lingerie designs, I'm keen on keeping that to myself.

"Well, then Daniella, you've got pretty reasonable demands, along with exquisite taste." I look away, freeing myself from her glower, and adjust the collar on my shirt. "Jonah will provide a computer flash drive that contains footage of the last few years of The Fashion Show as well as the catalog—per your request." I look to Jonah for confirmation.

"Oh, right. Of course. I'll just grab those from my office—just give me a few minutes to gather it all. Can I get you two anything while you wait? Water? Coffee?"

"No thanks," Daniella and I reply in unison.

Jonah excuses himself, leaving Daniella and me alone. The silence between the two of us is deafening. She sits, arms still folded, legs firmly crossed, a purposeful gaze toward the wall.

"You're angry."

"Annoyed," she clarifies.

"Are you always gonna be annoyed with me?"

"Are you always gonna rise to the occasion?"

"Without a doubt," I say, a droll attempt at easing the tension.

She faces me, eyes gleaming, and a sugary smile finally escapes her presumably tenacious nature.

It's then that I realize Jonah's right: Daniella Belle is indeed what I've been missing this whole time.

CHAPTER 10

DANIELLA

"So…are you actually going to Milan? With Antonio *he's-so-hot* Michaels?" clamors Emma via my computer screen on a FaceTime call.

She calls to *check up* on me about three times a day whenever she's away with her dad, mainly out of boredom, but I get the feeling Emma misses me every time we are apart. She's truly like the little sister I never had, but always wished for.

Peering up from the catalog of *CraveMe* lingerie items I've been perusing for the past hour, I grin. "Apparently, I am."

"Oh. My. God. You've *so* gotta convince my mom to allow you to take me with you, D! Tell her it's for a school project or something."

"No can do, babe. Plus, it's your last year of high school. You'd better savor every precious moment."

Emma sulks, as she crams a handful of potato chips into her mouth. "Fine. Just bring me home some Italian chocolate."

I chuckle at her demand. "You've got it."

"How was your first day as a PA? Is your new boss as dreamy as he looks?"

How about despicable, pretentious, and apathetic—all accentuated by mesmerizing charisma.

"Totally," I utter, knowing I'll never fool Emma since Little Miss All-Knowing does discern me quite well.

"Name one thing you like about him." She studies my expression as she takes a sip of soda.

"Excuse me?" I blink.

"My mom always says it helps to name at least one good thing about someone you don't particularly like."

Just what I need: unsolicited advice from a sixteen-year-old.

Reluctantly, I search deep into the pit of my gut, for something—anything—I like about Antonio.

"His smile," I finally decide.

Emma folds her arms and squints her expressive brown eyes. "Uh-huh. The two of you will be sending out wedding invitations upon your return from *Milan*."

I shake my head. "Nope. I think he's married."

"Married? No way! He's been seen out on dates with too many women, D…so nice try."

"Well…he's utterly impossible."

"So are you."

"He's stubborn."

"And, you're not?" She gleams at my annoyance.

"We are Night and Day."

"Opposites attract." She sticks out her tongue.

"Don't you have homework…or something?"

"Yep. In fact, I've got an assignment that's due in a couple of weeks. Maybe you can help?" She grins like the Cheshire Cat.

"And what exactly is this *assignment*?" I proceed with caution, knowing Emma always has a prank up her sleeve.

"I've gotta study Milan fashion shows and their impact on society—in Milan."

I can see the corners of Emma's mouth twitch, an obvious

struggle at holding back a giggle. Five seconds later, she cackles uncontrollably.

"You're funny," I say, semi-amused. "But seriously, get off this call and do your homework," I inject as a reminder that I'm still the adult here. "Besides, I'm kind of working on a small project, hon."

"Work-related?" she asks, her voice inflated, eyes widened.

"Yep. I promise to fill you in tomorrow."

Emma's expression softens. "Okay then, I'm off to do my homework. Good luck with your project. Love ya."

"I love ya too, babe."

Describing this project as small wasn't exactly a fitting characterization—more like mammoth.

Taking a hearty sip of hot peppermint tea, I retrieve a spiral notebook from my desk drawer and begin jotting down mental notes I made earlier while viewing the extensive video footage Jonah provided me. Apparently, the entire lingerie event in Milan is colossal—commencing with a grandiose fashion show and concluding with a ceremonial ball. Invitees of The Ball exclusively don the newest and hottest *avant-garde* creations by the fashion show's designers.

During the brainstorming meeting, I remember Antonio mentioned *CraveMe* has fallen behind compared to what other designers present on the catwalk. Seems they've been going all out, presumably trying to outdo the other, in an effort to leave a memorable impression. And from what I've seen on the videos, he's absolutely right. DJs, strobe lights, acrobatics, all in addition to an assortment of dazzling, *ass-baring*, women. It's no wonder Jonah is freaked-the-fuck out about the amount of time we have left to plan. There is no way *CraveMe* can expect to pull off anything close to what the others have—unless we decide, like yesterday, what the theme will be.

I rock back and forth in my chair as I scan my bedroom

walls for inspiration. Over the years, I've been collecting and framing pictures of women wearing chic lingerie that I use to influence my own design creations. *CraveMe's* thirty-minute contribution to the Fashion Show needs to be more of an all-out experience. To draw out my creative muse, I switch on my MP3 player—it's still set to my 1980s playlist. I tap my ink pen on the hard, wooden surface of my desk and bob my head to the funky sound of The Eurythmics-*Sweet Dreams*, and before I know it, I'm up, moving about my room, dancing to the beat. Even though I wasn't born in the '80s, I still appreciate everything from the era. The music. The movies. The hair. And even some of the clothing. If someone could ingeniously figure out how to intertwine the best parts of the '80s, '90s, and today—

Holy fuck. That's it.

The concept smacks me with such blunt force, I trip as I scamper back to my chair.

Immediately I begin conducting an online search for images, articles, just about everything I'll need to create a poppin' slideshow to present to Antonio and Jonah tomorrow at Creative Solutions, Inc.

NEARLY TWO HOURS, TWO MP3 PLAY SETS, AND TWO GLASSES OF wine later, I stare, in awe, at what I've come up with. It's phenomenally perfect and I honestly can't wait until tomorrow—even though I'll have to. I power down my laptop and pack it up for the meeting and shimmy my way into the closet, still feeling giddy over my creativity. I'll need to wear something professionally eye-poppin' to the meeting.

Something Holly Golightly-ish minus the hat, of course.

My phone rings.

Shit. It's Antonio. He and I exchanged phone numbers earlier when he reminded me I need to be available twenty-four hours a day. And, no doubt, he's likely calling to tell me what type of coffee I need to bring him to the meeting tomorrow. I mean, isn't that the sort of stuff I'm to do as his PA? Pick up his coffee on the way to work? Honestly, we really haven't discussed my primary duties.

"Sir?" I answer, still searching for an outfit to wear.

"Sir? That actually has a nice ring to it. But I prefer Sir Antonio…you know, as long as you're tossing the word *Sir* around." I hear a soft chuckle escape him.

His voice is soothing and sweet over the phone, like a soft lullaby. *He can put me to sleep anytime.* Ooops. That's the two glasses of wine talking. I swear.

"To what do I owe the honor?" I'm sure there are thousands of women in Los Angeles who would *kill* to have Antonio Michaels call them at—I glance at the clock display on my phone—10:35 p.m.

"I was calling to see if you've been able to come up with any ideas. I figured you'd still be up…probably still brainstorming?"

I smirk into the phone. "I'm actually all done. And I won't be sharing anything with you until tomorrow at the meeting."

"Done? Well that's great. Can't you give me a teaser?"

I let out an exaggerated sigh. "That will be a, no." I pull a black dress off of its hanger and hold it up against me while looking in the mirror.

He laughs. "Fair enough, Daniella Belle. What kind of coffee can I bring you?"

I stand up tall. "Um, me?" I stammer. "What coffee can you bring *me*?" *Isn't that what I'm supposed to be asking him?* I slouch down, my butt on the edge of one of my shoe shelves.

"Yes. I thought I'd get us some coffee on my way to pick you up. I figure since we live only a few miles apart and are both going to the same place tomorrow, we should go together. It will give us time to…talk."

My mouth opens, but nothing comes out. I wasn't

expecting him to pick up coffee nor was I expecting a ride. I even planned to Uber. Audible words are held hostage by the shock of him being…pleasant. Or maybe he's just being an efficient boss. Yep. That's it. Makes total sense.

"Okay," I finally manage to spill. "I'll take a cappuccino with whipped cream, please."

"Perfect. Plan to be ready to go by 7:45 sharp. Until tomorrow, Daniella. Sweet dreams."

CHAPTER 11

DANIELLA

T he doorbell rings at 7:45 a.m. sharp.

I've been feverishly waiting, fully dressed, since 6:30 a.m. I hardly slept last night, my mind greatly absorbed with thoughts of today. It'll be my first presentation, since design school—and frankly, I have no clue how Antonio and Jonah are going to react to my suggestions.

I examine my reflection in the floor-length mirror that clings perfectly to the wall by the front door.

Hair done up in an Audrey Hepburn bun—which, on its own, took over an hour to perfect.

Black dress. Black heels. Red lipstick.

Yep. I'm good.

I peek into my leather tote, scanning its contents.

Phone. Wallet. Lipstick. Mascara. Laptop.

Yep. It's all there.

Taking in a calming deep breath, I clutch the leather tote bag, flinging it on my shoulder, and swing the door open, fully prepared to flash Antonio an *oh it's only you* look.

Then, like a groupie, I nearly pass out.

Without a single measure of doubt, Antonio Michaels seems to grow yummier-looking.

Every. Single. Day.

"You're ready?" he says, eyebrows raised.

"You're surprised?" I step out, closing and locking the door behind me.

"Well, in my experience, most ladies are never ready on time." He simpers, as if he's the only man in the world who's come to that absurd conclusion.

"Perhaps I'm not most ladies," I propose.

"Indeed, you're not." He winks and the two of us walk side by side toward his silver Mercedes. Like a gentleman, Antonio opens the passenger door. "Buckle up please, Miss Personal Assistant."

Honoring his command, I dutifully slide into the sleek leather seat and buckle up. The scent of his cologne consumes the atmosphere, and for a nanosecond my–ahem–lady bit, is overcome by salacious desire. I cross my legs, and sternly put her in check with a reprimanding *don't you dare go there, miss thang*.

The moment we hit the road, Antonio points to my cappuccino sitting in the cup holder. "I didn't picture you to be the cappuccino with whipped cream kind of girl. I thought for sure you'd order something far more intricate."

"Judgmental?"

A skittish smile tugs at his lips as though they are bracing for his imminent quip. "*That* inquiry coming from the woman who called me a first-class jerk on the Metro?"

I twirl a loose strand of my hair. "Alrighty then…how do you take yours?"

He turns to face me, heady gaze fixed on mine. "Hot. Smooth. Creamy." His robust tone is as alluring as his assertion.

Heat curls down my spine and I nearly melt into the passenger seat. He is talking about coffee, right?

We sip our respective cups of java in silence as Antonio zips along Wilshire Blvd, its sidewalks already riddled with a wide assortment of pedestrians. Hurried businessmen in stuffy suits racing to their meetings. Older ladies wandering aimlessly as they haul their carts full of groceries. Meter Maids issuing parking tickets. It's like a people watcher's dream.

The car crawls to a brief stop at a traffic light, and even though I'm avoiding eye contact, clearly trying to cool off from his off-putting comment, I can feel his gaze upon me. "What's your specialty?" he asks.

I turn my head abruptly to face him. "I'm sorry?" I answer, feeling a tad thrown off.

"You went to design school so, what's your area of specialty?"

Oh. Right. He's talking *that* kind of specialty. Duh. I'll need just a teeny-tiny minute while I get my head out of the gutter.

After taking a sip of my cappuccino, I finally mutter. "Lingerie."

One eyebrow raised, he says, "Seriously? I would have never guessed lingerie. But I would have guessed dresses and shoes. From what I've seen you wear so far, you have elaborate taste."

Is he flirting? Or just passing down a genuine compliment? I think back to the photo of the young pregnant woman I saw on his office desk yesterday and, with that in mind, I dismiss the thought of him flirting.

"Well, thanks. I started off designing dresses, actually. When I was much younger, of course. But, as I got older, I began sketching lingerie pieces. After I got accepted into design school, I focused solely on lingerie."

He offers a smile, but his expression is somewhat vacant, leaving me to ponder whether he's impressed or not.

Antonio pulls into the Creative Solutions, Inc complex and maneuvers his way through the underground parking garage until he eases the Benz in-between two parked cars. "I'm glad we had a little time to chat, Daniella, and honestly, I can't wait to see the ideas you've come up with."

Up in the boardroom, Jonah greets us, offering breakfast pastries, fruit, and yogurt. He rubs his hands together as he looks at me and smiles. "Are you ready to rock and roll? If you've got a presentation, I'll gladly connect your laptop to the projector."

I place my tote onto the large table and remove my laptop. "Sure thing," I say, feeling my heart rate speed up as the realization of me *actually* presenting, now, in real-fucking-time, kicks in.

Jonah takes my laptop while I slowly ease down into a seat next to Antonio's.

"You okay?" Antonio asks.

I bite on my lower lip. "Of course."

He smiles, leaning in close, and whispers into my ear, "Don't be nervous—Jonah and I are really looking forward to this presentation."

"I'll be fine, thanks," I affirm, knowing damn well that's a straight-out lie.

"Okay, you're set, Daniella. The floor's all yours," Jonah says, as he encouragingly claps his hands, claiming a seat across from Antonio.

Buying time, I slowly tug my butt out of the seat, smoothing down my dress as I rise to a knee-wobbly stance. Inching my way toward the laptop to load the presentation onto the projection screen, I mentally recap the talking points of my proposal.

Breathe, Daniella Belle. Just breathe.

CHAPTER 12

ANTONIO

She's nervous.

I pretty much surmised that the moment she flung the door open to greet me—her frazzled green eyes resisting my eager gaze.

If she were mine, I would have scooped her up in my arms and—

What the hell does it matter? She's *not* mine. Women like her won't give someone like me the time of day. Instead, I attract women who are on a fast track mission toward fame and fortune.

Can I be in a CraveMe *commercial? What about the* CraveMe *catalog?* Or *Can you introduce me to a movie producer?* As if I've got *quid pro quo* tattooed across my chest.

It's no wonder I've never been in love—though it's not like I haven't tried. God knows I have. Yet, the struggle to find someone interested in *just* me is real.

I know, I know…boo-freaking-hoo for the handsome rich guy who can't find love, right?

I can't help but think Daniella could very well be the *one*. It's an indisputable sensation I get each time I lay eyes on her.

Not a carnal sensation; well yeah, I'm not gonna lie—that too. I mean seriously, she is felicitously hot.

Whenever I lay my eyes on her, I see a woman who's meant for me; although I am not sure why, exactly.

"Okay," Daniella speaks softly as she stands behind her laptop that's propped on the end of the large oval-shaped boardroom table. She bites on her bottom lip. "Jonah, will you please turn the lights down?"

Jonah lifts a small remote control off the table and forcefully points it to the ceiling, effectively dimming the lights. He offers Daniella two thumbs up and says, "Mission accomplished."

She looks at Jonah then to me; an intrepid smile emerges, complementing her flawless features. "Gentlemen, brace yourself for *Get Your Chic On—A Tribute To Confident Women."*

Stepping to the side, Daniella fans out one arm, gesturing us to divert our attention to the large projection screen. "Women. They make up eighty percent of those who purchase lingerie."

Scrolling across the screen are images of women donning provocative lingerie, as they stand in front of a mirror, seductively studying their own reflection.

With one hand on her hip and one sexy-as-hell, stiletto-enhanced foot jutted out, Daniella goes on. "And why is that? It's simple. In order to be sexy, a woman must first *feel* sexy. And feeling sexy exudes more than simple allurement. Sexy exudes confidence." She pivots, and begins pacing back and forth in front of the projection screen. "Confidence to conquer the day. Confidence to ace that job interview. Confidence to boost up her self-esteem when she's feeling a little down. And of course…confidence to please her man."

Jonah leans back in his seat, placing his Nike-covered feet up on the table, and grins. "Well, all right, now! I think I like where this is headed."

I chuckle at his enthusiasm, then lean forward in my seat, giving Daniella my undivided attention.

She places both hands on the table and leans forward with a resolute gaze glued to me and Jonah. "Gentlemen, what better way to showcase *CraveMe* than with beautifully confident women, strutting down the catwalk, wearing an assortment of *CraveMe* pieces—from elegant designs to naughty designs."

My eyebrows rise with interest all on their own.

"Our models will tastefully prance the runway," she continues, "to music from an era in which ladies vocalized songs with just the right blend of bad-assery and sassy confidence."

Jonah nods. "And from what musical era would that be, exactly?"

Daniella stands tall, arms folded as she brandishes an audacious smirk. "The 1980s."

Jonah smiles, while I internally cringe.

She takes a few steps toward her seat and spills into it. "Think about it. Female pop vocalists of the '80s were strong and confident with fierce vocals that were packed with messages of empowerment. These women came across as being in charge of their own destiny, and that confidence made them sexy without being *just* sexy. We can give models big '80s hair and makeup. Some dressed only in *CraveMe* pieces, while others will be dressed in clothes with *CraveMe* pieces underneath. For instance, imagine Donna Summer's *She Works Hard For The Money* blaring in the background. Our models swagger along the walk, briefcases in hand, sleek hair pulled back, eyeglasses, dressed in tight miniskirts and a formfitting blazer; only, underneath the blazer is a very prominent *CraveMe* bra."

Silence consumes the room for a brief second.

Jonah stands and claps his hands. "Now *this* is a woman

who knows her shit. Antonio, you must admit this is freaking gold right here."

I rock back and forth in my chair as I rub the small amount of stubble growing along my chin. I really can't stand music from the '80s—and Jonah of all people knows this all too well. Nonetheless, what Daniella suggests may just work. If we add the right amount of lighting and match the right pieces with the right songs, this could be *CraveMe's* knock-it-out-of-the-park year in Milan.

I sit up in my chair and look to Daniella whose confidence seems to be dwindling, most likely due to my silence. "Great job. I love it. Even if '80s music isn't typically my thing."

Jonah cackles at the last part of my comment and plops back down in his seat.

"But, I think if you and I match the right piece with the right song, this, as Jonah put it, will be gold."

Daniella's cheeks redden. "I'm so glad you think so. And thank you for allowing me the chance to share my idea with you both."

"So, will the new pieces you designed this year fit this *Confident Woman* theme?" Jonah asks.

I give a half-shrug. "I dunno. Maybe. I'm actually not quite sure. They just came in last week and I haven't bothered to look at them yet. I've been preoccupied," I hastily admit.

Although, I should have made time already. Every year, I design new pieces of lingerie that are to be debuted first in Milan. I know I should be better prepared.

"Well, where are they? Let's have a look."

I scoff. Not at Jonah's inquisition, but at my own damn self. "I left the boxes at home. I meant to throw them in the car, but forgot."

Truth is, I was so excited to pick up Daniella, I left the boxes of newly designed pieces on my kitchen table. Yes, I'm a complete idiot.

"We can go get them, right?" Daniella softly interjects.

"That's a great idea," Jonah says, glancing at his watch. "But you two go right on. I have three more clients I'm meeting with today." He gets up and pushes in his chair. "Great job, Daniella. I look forward to working with you."

Daniella stands with her hands behind her back. "Thanks! Same here."

"So, are you sure you don't mind going with me to pick up the designs?" I ask Daniella.

"Oh, not at all, boss. I'm beyond elated that I get to see them!"

CHAPTER 13

DANIELLA

I was nervous as fuck, however I doubt neither Antonio nor Jonah noticed. In fact, I rocked the hell out of that presentation and, as soon as I get home, I'm totally making waffles to celebrate.

It's been a pretty quiet ride to Antonio's house as he and I both seem to be consumed by our own private thoughts. Me, over the excitement of helping plan the fashion show. But I'm not certain I'd be able to guess what's on Antonio's mind. He's a bit mysterious, honestly. Although, in his defense, that's the case with most creative types. Lord knows, I've been referred to as mysterious plenty of times.

Stealing a surreptitious glance, I try to study his expression.

Fail.

I can't make out a damn thing through his dark sunglasses.

Mysterious or not, I'm thankful for the opportunity to work with him. He seems to be less of a jerk to me with each passing day.

He turns onto Sunset Blvd and drives west before coming to a crawl approaching a black iron gate.

Antonio slides his designer shades on to the top of his perfectly styled hair. "We're here. My humble abode."

The gate creeps open, and Antonio zips through the opening and up a long cobblestone-lined driveway before parking at a hasty angle in front of a row of three garage doors. And to the left of the garage doors sits a stunning, white, two-story, Mediterranean-style villa.

He kills the engine and jumps out of the car, wanders over to my side, and opens my door. He leans in slightly. "Um, Daniella...you okay?"

A fleeting pause lingers between us as I stare, in awe, at his house.

"Yeah, sure. It's just...your house. It's gorgeous."

He lifts a brow and chuckles. "It's all right." He takes my hand, politely aiding me, as I step out of the car and onto the driveway. "Come on. I'll give you the grand tour."

The two of us climb a flight of stairs, leading up to the embossed double-door entry.

"Holy shit, Antonio," I let out the instant we're inside. The entry hall is majestic, showcasing a grand sweeping staircase.

He slides my tote bag off my shoulder and hangs it on the coat rack by the doorway. "People have said many things as they walk in...but I'll grant you none have said *holy shit*."

His blue eyes brighten as he stands in front of me, peering down to meet my gaze. He's much taller than I am, even while wearing these five-inch stilettos, that are actually killing me right now.

"Mind if I remove my shoes?" I say, just as I begin to extract myself from them.

He opens his mouth to answer, but I'm already barefoot, playfully wiggling my newly manicured toes, as I stand before him more miniature-sized than I was only seconds ago.

"Not at all and...nice toes." He laughs. "C'mon. Let's begin the tour."

He gestures for me to follow and I do so, allowing my

eyes to scan the sophisticated, yet modern, décor of all things black and white.

My feet feel cold walking behind him on the marble floor, as we trek past an ebony-colored, rectangular accent table that holds a small collection of crystal vases. Above the table hangs a large, framed black-and-white photo-collage of famous Hollywood movie directors. I feel my stare widen as I walk past it, then I bump into the backside of Antonio, who has apparently stopped at the base of the sweeping staircase.

Turning around to face me, Antonio grabs hold of my arms, his grip soft yet firm, as I clumsily lose my footing. "Whoops. You okay? Lucky for you I'm not holding a jelly donut this time." He looks down at me and winks when our eyes meet. "I, uh, figure we can begin your tour upstairs, then finish downstairs before we look at the designs."

I nod in anticipation as excitement, as well as total embarrassment, has captured my ability to speak.

Upstairs, Antonio takes me through six bedrooms and four bathrooms, all decorated in the elaborate black-and-white theme that I've now gathered is flourished about the entire home. Most of the bedrooms have windows with magnificent views of nearby Century City and the Pacific Ocean.

We come to a double door and, before opening, Antonio explains. "This is my room, so please excuse the mess." His mouth slips into a playful grin as he goes on. "The bed is never made and—"

"Antonio. Seriously? It's just a bedroom." I laugh at his spiel and roll my eyes. Then turn the doorknob and let myself in.

My eyes survey the space that has to be at least a thousand square feet.

Gorgeous. Huge. Dreamy.

A king-sized bed that is indeed unmade, but still cozy looking.

A 50-inch TV that hangs over the wood-burning fireplace.

A large deck with a wet bar and jacuzzi.

Two walk-in closets.

And a bathroom with a step-in Spanish-tiled shower equipped with six shower heads, and to the right of that, a bathtub large enough to bathe an army.

Antonio busies himself, picking up loose articles of clothing from off the floor. "I wasn't exactly expecting company." His cheeks turn red—and it's the first time the cool and collected Antonio seems nervous.

He's actually human, after all.

I feel a satisfying grin devour my face and, while I try to hide my amusement, my grin doesn't go unnoticed.

Antonio tosses an armful of clothing into one of the closets. "And what is it you find so funny?" he solicits, armed with his own mirthful simper.

"Truthfully, I find it kind of cute you're embarrassed that your room is a little messy."

"Cute? Well I guess that's something." He places his hand along the small of my back, the contact causing my heart to jump. "How about I show you the rest of the house?"

I giggle as I'm guided out of his room. "Of course. I'd love to see more."

Back downstairs, Antonio presents a dining room, a grand living room overlooking a flower garden, an office, a thirteen-seat theater room, an elaborate kitchen, and a unique outdoor living room, before he escorts me into the library—the only room in the house that is not shrouded in black-and-white décor. It's rather large in scale, with ginger-colored walls and floor-to-ceiling shelves displaying an assortment of books.

Besides the shelves being the focal point of the room, there is a rustic-looking brick fireplace. Sitting on its mantel is a large black-and-white photo. The same photo that sits on his desk back at his office, only obviously much larger.

I walk over to take a closer look and, as I stand there,

admiring the ravishing woman, curiosity gets the best of me. "Is this your wife, Antonio? She's strikingly beautiful."

He clears his throat. "My wife? Uh, no. I'm not at all married." He stands beside me, appearing to also admire the woman in the photo. "She," he explains, now pointing to the photo, "was my dear mother. I had her photo restored."

Now, that I wasn't expecting.

"*Was* your mother?"

He nods. "Yep. Unfortunately, I never met her. She died shortly after I was born—this is a photograph of her when she was pregnant with me. I cherish it and display it in here, because my mom loved to read. My grandma told me my mother read to me every single day while she was pregnant."

I shake my head in utter despair. "I'm sorry, Antonio, I had no idea."

"It's okay," he says. "Not that many people do know...I don't typically show anyone this room, really. And it's unusual for me to feel comfortable enough to even talk about my mother." He grabs hold of my hand, leading me out of the room, and closes the door behind us. "How about we head to the kitchen to check out those designs now?"

I nod, thinking it's really the only appropriate response.

In the kitchen, Antonio breaks the silence that stood between us as we walked from the library into the kitchen. He invites me to sit down on one of the chairs surrounding the rectangular dining table.

"Would you care for something to drink, Daniella? I can make coffee, offer you a bottle of water, a martini, or—"

"A martini?" I snicker. "I'm on the clock, Sir."

He looks up from an invoice he's reading. "Yes, but you're with the boss, so it doesn't count," he quips. "But you're right. I'll show off my liquid chef skills to you another time."

"Liquid chef?"

"Yes. I'm quite talented in the mixed drinks department.

So much so, my talent extends beyond that of a bartender or mixologist."

"So, because of said talent, you refer to yourself as a liquid chef?" I ask, clearly amused.

One eyebrow raised, Antonio says, "Among other things."

"Fine." I fold my arms over my chest and squint my eyes. "Indulge me. I'll gladly take a martini, please."

His eyes glisten and the corner of his mouth lifts. "Shaken or stirred?"

CHAPTER 14

ANTONIO

It's not often I get to show off my liquid chef skills. My life is way too busy for anything social. In fact, Daniella is the first woman I've brought home in a long time. Sure, the stories on the news and on Internet sites peg me as this modern-day Casanova type with the flashy car and swanky models at my side. The thing is, those photo and video ops are strategically planned out—campaigns carried out by Jonah's marketing firm and his public relations team. They presume, as the CEO of a sexy lingerie line, my lifestyle should be portrayed as incredibly sumptuous.

But it's not.

The last woman I dated was the crazy one who, after I broke up with her, rented a billboard in Hollywood displaying my home address. As it stands now, I don't even have a date for The Lingerie Ball.

Daniella sits across from me at the outdoor bar in my backyard, with a pensive glow in her eyes, watching as I put on my best bartender performance—I'm Brian Flanagan and she's Jordan Mooney—from the movie *Cocktail*. Don't judge me. That movie really is a dick flick disguised as a chick flick.

With a cocktail shaker in hand, I add ice, gin—only a little because I don't want her tipsy—I am a gentleman after all—and a splash of vermouth, then place the strainer over the top. With one hand gripping the shaker and both eyes on Daniella, I shake it for a few seconds then pour the contents into a martini glass, adding what I guess to be her preferred garnish.

Sliding the glass over to her I say, "Madam? Your drink is served."

She tilts her head to the side and lifts the glass to the base of her heart-shaped lips. "And just how did you know I take mine with a twist of lemon?"

"Lucky guess? Taste it."

Her lips grip the rim of the glass and she closes her eyes momentarily, taking a sip. "Mmmm, Antonio. It's quite lovely. It's actually been a while since I've had a martini. You make a fine one, Mr. Liquid Chef."

"That's *Sir* Liquid Chef," I tease. "I'm glad you like it."

After making a martini for myself, I slide onto the barstool next to Daniella and hold up my glass to hers. "Cheers to a fabulous start to our working relationship."

She smiles, taking another sip of her drink before placing the glass down on the countertop. She looks down, deep in thought, her index finger tracing the rim of her glass, its fingernail painted the same pink color as her toenails.

Her legs are crossed and being this close to her, I can't help but notice how sexy they are.

Tan. Smooth. Erogenous.

Am I a horrible boss for wanting her as badly as I do?

Probably.

"Hey, are you hungry?" I ask, mainly to take my mind off her hotness. "I'm no Emeril Legassi, but I can make a mean salami sandwich."

She finally looks up from the glass she's been pensively tracing, a snicker framing her face. "Salami?"

I shrug. "It's the only thing I've got in the fridge."

"You don't have like your own personal chef?"

"Nah. No personal chef. Not even a housekeeper."

Daniella slides off the barstool, planting her bare feet onto the stone paved patio floor. She steps over to me and grabs hold of my necktie, gesturing for me to stand.

"Antonio Michaels, you're not at all the man I envisioned you to be. And yes, I'd actually love a salami sandwich, please."

"Your wish is my command. And after that, we'll definitely look at the designs."

۞

DANIELLA AND I CHAT ABOUT HER RELATIONSHIP WITH EMMA and Stacy while we gulp down sandwiches and the rest of our martinis. She explained the two are her only real sense of family, as she grew up in a foster home in Texas and took off for Los Angeles, with money she had saved up, as soon as she turned eighteen. I guess we both unexpectedly learned a lot about each other today.

"How about we peek at the designs now?" I propose, removing our plates and glasses from the table and placing them in the dishwasher.

"Yes. I'd love that." Her eyes brighten like a little girl who received a pony on her birthday.

"Now allow me to reiterate: this will be my first time seeing these designs since they came back from the factory in Milan," I explain as I tear into the box.

"*CraveMe* pieces are made in Milan?"

I nod. "Most of them, in Bergamo. I have an uncle who owns a boutique and a small garment factory. A few *CraveMe* pieces are sold in his boutique—he keeps the profits, in exchange for making the clothes he sends here."

"Oh, I see. That's a pretty neat setup."

"It is. Only it also requires me to spend a great deal of my time in Milan as well. I prefer to handpick the fabric, especially for new designs. This time around, I didn't have time to go, so I relied on my uncle to choose the fabric. Maybe that's why I've been putting off looking at how they turned out. I'm nervous."

Daniella bites on her lower lip. "And if you're not particularly happy with them?"

"Haven't thought about that yet." I remove the protective wrap and mentally brace myself. "You ready?"

She stands on her toes, peering over the open box in anticipation. "Yes."

Removing each piece, one by one, I place them in a pile in the middle of the table. Daniella seems beside herself, eyes widened, clearly intrigued by this unveiling. There are panties, bras, camisoles, negligees, and teddies, in an array of colors, all made of sheer fabric. I wanted to go bold this year.

Daniella begins to sift through them and the look on her face makes me nervous.

"What do you think?"

She holds up a bra and raises her eyebrows. "They're kind of see-through," she says, her gorgeous green eyes flashing with shock.

"Yep. I'm going for bold this year. Which I think ties into the Confident Women theme you presented. If a woman can rock these, she'll feel as though she can conquer the world, no?"

"Sure, I suppose. But remember, women wear lingerie for themselves, first and foremost. These kind of look like they were meant to be purchased by a man for his woman to wear seconds before he rips them off her and pours into her. Which is fine...but not at all what a woman would wear every day. Does that make sense?"

I sit down now, lifting one of the bras up to inspect it. To me they are perfect. But she seems less impressed than I am.

"So you view my lingerie as something a woman wears only for her man?"

She nods. "Sort of."

"Yesterday you told me you were wearing some when we were in the boardroom. Clearly that was not a wear-them-for-your-man moment." I feel my mouth curve into a playful smirk at the sight of her brightened face.

"Well, yeah," she stammers. "I'd bought several *CraveMe* pieces long ago, and never wore them. I thought it only fitting to conduct hands-on product research my first day on the job."

"And? How did they make you feel?"

She looks away for a moment before meeting my gaze. "Amazingly hot."

"Plus a little confident, perhaps? I mean, you were able to convince me to give you a stab at presenting your idea for the fashion show. You seemed pretty damn confident to me, if you don't mind me saying so."

She tosses a bra at me and smiles. "Fine. You made your point." She scoffs. "But in my defense, the bra and panties I wore yesterday, were not like these. They were less…revealing. Perhaps make a few adjustments? Leave some parts covered?"

"Fair enough. We'll need to go to Milan a week ahead of the event anyway to prepare. I can enhance some of the designs then. Maybe even come up with some additional designs. My uncle is great for a quick turnaround."

"Um, *we* need to be there a week ahead?"

"Yep. I mentioned during your interview, you'll be going to Milan as well, and you'll attend both events—the Fashion Show and The Ball. I need to arrive about a week early and, as my assistant, I really want you with me."

"So, um, when do we leave?" She lowers herself into the seat.

"Sunday." I peer up and catch a glimpse of her rosy cheeks and dropped jaw.

"As in three days from now?"

"Yep. I've already booked your airfare and hotel."

"Isn't it cold in Milan this time of year?" Her breathing quickens as if she's becoming a tad panicked. "I don't even have—"

"Daniella," I softly interrupt and her breathing begins to return to normal. "Yes, it is cold this time of year in Milan. But you'll have the rest of the week to shop for clothes. Since it's work related, the shopping is on me."

She looks at me, her eyes much calmer now. "I was only going to say I don't even have time to pack for a trip so grand."

She leaps up from her seat, and takes a giant step over to me, throwing her arms around my neck, hugging me as if I were her very own teddy bear. "Oh, Antonio, I'm so thrilled I get to go to Milan!"

She pulls away—the hug, feeling her that close, along with the intoxicating whiff of her perfume, makes my heart dance.

"I'm happy you're thrilled. But it's going to be a lot of work since I'm way behind."

She nods. "We can make it work, Antonio. Like I said before, I'm your girl."

If only she knew…

CHAPTER 15

DANIELLA

Ecstatic.

The only way I can accurately describe how I'm feeling, as I toss and turn, trying my hardest to will myself asleep. I've been mentally scanning multiple checklists, ensuring I packed everything needed for the almost ten-day trip to Milan.

Milan! The fashion. The food. The totality.

Antonio gave me the rest of the week off to shop and prepare for the trip. Admittedly, I've been running around Los Angeles like a mad woman, sorting things out. Not to mention, I spent two—painstaking hours—searching for my passport that I eventually found tucked away in one of my suitcases.

It's Saturday night now, and even though butterflies have swarmed my giddy-filled gut, I'm also kind of bummed I won't get to see Emma and Stacy before I leave early tomorrow morning.

Emma has called me at least forty-seven times today. She seems obviously more thrilled than I am, with a twisted notion that somehow Antonio and I will return from this trip as a 'happier than ever' couple. Stacy hasn't helped either, as she, like a fucking parrot, keeps saying over and over how Antonio is fresh-out-of-the-bakery *hot*.

That, of course, I can't deny.

Personally, I think the two of them watch way too many of those damn Hallmark movies. Sappy romance bullshit, if you ask me.

I'm sticking to my pledge of swearing off men.

Plus, the fact that Antonio revealed he is not at all married only led me back to the notion that he, like a snug glove, fits the bill of a lady lovin' playboy. That is, at least according to my highly reputable source known as Google—honestly, all searches annoyingly point to images of him with a different woman every month. All that was solidified when he dropped me off at home the other day, after we looked at the designs from Milan. His phone showed an incoming call from someone named *Nonna*. A name like that is probably attached to a slinky lingerie model with big boobs and a flat ass.

Yet, I suppose if I had his money and semi-fame, I'd probably live life to the fullest too, before ever settling down.

He's actually growing on me—the way a bad haircut does. He's much kinder than I expected, and I feel bad that he lost his mom; although, I have yet to uncover the complete details as Google shows nothing related to that. I dare not ask. I dare not intrude.

I am a tad nervous about spending nearly two weeks with him whether it's work-related or not. Luckily, it won't be just the two of us for the entire trip. Liza, his receptionist, and Jonah will be coming to Milan as well, albeit not until several days later. Jonah apparently goes each year, and this year, Antonio rewarded Liza the trip for helping him out when his PA, Dottie, retired.

Looking at the digital clock that sits on my bedside table, I see it brightly displays it's nearly midnight. Only four more hours until the alarm rings. I stuck my phone under my pillow so I'd be sure to hear its alarm when it goes off. It would be a tragedy if I slept through the alarm. It's not like that hasn't happened to me before—too many times to count, actually. Like the time I—

My phone just chimed. No one in their right mind would text me this late. Not even a booty call, which incidentally, I've never experienced, so what do I know about booty calls?

I stick my hand under the pillow, grabbing my phone, squinting as I try to read the screen.

It's Antonio.

I sit up in a panic.

What if the flight is cancelled? Or worse, what if he's cancelled the entire trip for some odd reason?

I'm almost too afraid to look.

Oh just look, damn it.

Antonio: **Hey, are you awake? If not, no worries. I'll just see you tomorrow morning.**

I cover my mouth, stifling my giggle.

Me: **And what if I weren't awake, but am now because of your text?**

A pause ceases the moment.

Antonio: **Why are you always such a smarty pants?**

Me: **Smarty pants? Are we back in grade school?**

He replies with an emoji sticking out its tongue.

Me: **That's real cute. Kind of looks like you, too.**

Antonio: **I can't sleep so I thought I'd see if you're having trouble sleeping too.**

Me: **I'm too excited to sleep.**

Antonio: **I'm happy you're excited. But sleep, Daniella Belle. I'll pick you up at 5 a.m. sharp. Sweet dreams.**

Me: **Sweet dreams.**

I did it.

Slept right through my fucking alarm—awakened only by

the grace of Antonio sending me a courtesy text to tell me he's on his way to my house.

I leapt out of bed, ran into the bathroom, washed my face, brushed my teeth, and threw my hair in what is supposed to be a ponytail, before I slipped into a bra and panty, blue skinny jeans, and a black *CraveMe* T-shirt I found on sale in a little boutique on Rodeo Drive.

There was no time at all for mascara, but I did manage to dab on some bright pink lip gloss before the doorbell rang.

And now I'm standing here, judging my reflection in the mirror, before I turn the doorknob.

"Nice shirt. That is part of a new casual line we're testing. It looks amazing on you. You all set?" a slammin' Antonio says when I swing the door open.

I mean, why does the man have to look so damn good?

"Yep. I just need help with my bags." He looks at all three suitcases and laughs. "Are you *moving* to Milan?"

"That's not a bad idea," I cheekily retort.

"I'm getting used to your sarcasm, Miss Personal Assistant."

"Great. Then I'll be sure to toss more your way, every chance I get."

Impressive biceps in both arms swell prominently as he lifts two of the suitcases. "I didn't say I enjoy it."

"Then why are you smiling?"

Our eyes briefly lock as he licks his lips when he slowly walks past me. A subtle hint of his cologne sends chills up and down my spine. "Miss Belle, we need to hurry. And grab a light jacket. It's a little brisk outside. Oh, and a pair of sunglasses."

"Sunglasses?"

"Uh, yeah," he says, setting down the suitcases outside. "TMZ loves to hang out at the airport. Dark sunglasses will shield your face and spare you a media frenzy." I watch his lips transform into a coquettish smirk. "Unless, of course, you're into that sort of thing."

Uh, no.

"I have sunglasses in my purse," I retort.

Antonio loads my suitcases into the backseat of his car as I grab a jacket and lock up the house.

And before I know it, he speeds off toward Los Angeles International Airport.

Milan…here we come.

CHAPTER 16

DANIELLA

"**L**adies and Gentlemen, we'd like to welcome you on board Flight 2811 with service from Los Angeles to New York, then continuing on to Milan, Italy. We are currently third in line for takeoff and should be in the air in approximately eight minutes…"

After the flight attendant's lengthy announcement, she takes in a deep breath before placing the receiver back onto its hook. With burgundy-lipstick-coated, pursed lips, she walks down the aisle, shifting her gaze from left to right, dutifully inspecting each passenger's safety belt, ensuring they have all followed the instructions she blared over the PA.

First Class.

I've never been on board an airplane, experiencing the luxury of first class; although, I have walked through first class—on my way to the far end of the plane, of course.

I feel swanky.

Celebrity-ish.

Wait. Is that even a word?

Who cares?

A petite flight attendant hands Antonio and me a plastic

cup of orange juice each. "*Benvenuti a bordo,*" she says in a husky yet feminine tone.

I nod and Antonio smiles, offering a respectful, "*Grazie.*"

I elbow him gently on the side. "So…you speak Italian?" I sip my orange juice.

"Yep. Fluently. It helps, with me traveling so much to and from Milan."

How sexy is that?

"Oooh, that's intriguing," I say, shielding my true level of excitement. "I've always wanted to learn."

"Maybe I'll teach you."

Minutes later, the plane takes off and soon after, we're served breakfast, that incidentally, the two of us are just too tired to eat. We end up falling asleep while watching the complimentary movie and seem to simultaneously wake up, the moment the plane lands in New York City.

Antonio looks at me through sleepy, albeit playful, eyes. "Well, it looks as though we got sleeping together out of the way."

I can't help but laugh—thrown completely off by his unpredicted mirthfulness.

"I'm getting used to your shock-and-awe comments."

He stretches and catches my glance with his own extremely speculative eyes. "Really, now? I suppose that's good, but I'm still likely to throw you for a complete spin every now and then."

As the plane taxis to its assigned gate, the husky-sounding flight attendant announces that passengers continuing on to Milan should remain on board while the plane undergoes the refuel process and JFK passengers board.

Antonio and I both use the restroom and freshen up before the passenger boarding process begins and then we busy ourselves answering text messages and emails. I send selfies of myself to Emma and Stacy who both, in return, send me replies of similar *have a safe flight* content.

Antonio places his cell phone on the seat-back table while he reviews our itinerary. His phone vibrates—displaying a call from *Nonna*.

Ugh. I don't know why I cringe at her. I mean I don't even know the woman. I still suspect she's a slinky model. Someone he's involved with, for sure. Maybe I should Google her. I'm sure a model called *Nonna* is highly searchable—a famous one or two-namer like Madonna, Beyoncé, or Miss Piggy.

He answers the call, leaning into the phone with his voice lowered. *"Buongiorno, Nonna, sono sull'aereo."*

Fuck.

He's speaking Italian, of course.

Which means she's probably some Italian hottie he keeps around for his trips to and from Milan.

And there is no way I'll be able to understand a word he's saying to her.

Maybe if I listen close enough, I can make out at least one or two of the words. I mean, how difficult can it be, right?

Placing my elbow onto the armrest that sits between his seat and mine, I lean my face against the palm of my hand, pretending to be resting when I'm really trying to eavesdrop.

"Sì, Nonna. Sono davvero contento che domani ci vediamo." He smiles and blows a kiss into the phone. *"Ti adoro,"* he says before ending the call then placing the phone in the seat-back pocket.

Ti adoro? Isn't that like, *I adore you*?

Gag me.

He looks at me, his expression quizzical. "What?"

"Was that your girlfriend?" I offer a magnified grin.

"Who? Nonna? Uh—" he breaks off at the sound of the phone's echoing vibration. He removes it from the seat-back pocket and, with bunched eyebrows, looks at the screen. "It's Liza." He places the phone to his ear. "Hello?"

My curiosity piques.

Antonio nods a few times, fully engrossed in whatever Liza is saying on the other end of the phone. "Uh-huh. Well, great. That's all we need." He turns his head to face me, his dark-blues casting a look of annoyance that's invading his almost-too-perfect features. He continues his conversation. "Okay, send me a screenshot of the photo when it surfaces please. Thanks, Liza."

He ends the call, this time *shoving* his phone in the seatback pocket.

"Is everything all right?" I venture.

He shakes his head. "Apparently TMZ was doing what it does best—lurking at the airport. Liza says they claim to have captured a photo of me and *a beautiful woman* together, as we got onto the escalator toward the security checkpoint."

My eyes widen.

"Yep. I'm not sure what the photo looks like, but they love to spin stuff for publicity. I'm so sorry, Daniella. I hope the fact you had sunglasses on helped shield your identity. I would hate to have you all over the media again. Odds are, since they've probably gathered I'm on my way to Italy, there'll be more at the airport in Milan…waiting to snap more photos."

I place my hand on his forearm. "It's okay, really. Whatever they've got—or will get—should blow over soon enough."

He rubs his chin. "Right. The price of being a little popular, I guess. Still, I'd kill for a much more private life. I honestly don't know how the other designers manage to avoid paparazzi and inflated news stories."

"Maybe they don't have your looks and charm."

"Nor do they have the *beautiful woman* by their side?"

Heat rushes to my cheeks, and I shift my gaze from his sultry eyes to the window, reminding myself he's not flirting.

He's got *Nonna*.

A barrage of New York passengers board and, soon afterward, the plane pushes back and begins to taxi toward the runway. A different voice—this time a male with a brute Italian accent—takes on the pre-flight announcements and, before I know it, we are up in the air again.

After the pilot ascends the plane to the desired altitude, flight attendants begin to scurry about, preparing for beverage service. A slender flight attendant with mink-brown hair and a heavily made-up face approaches our seats. The cling-clang sound of her dangle bracelets sever the quietness in first class. She smiles at Antonio, placing her hand on his shoulder. "Antonio…it's always a pleasure to see you on board one of my flights."

Through gritted teeth Antonio replies, "Hello, Heather." He peels her hand off his shoulder. "'You're working first class today?"

Heather shifts to face us both, plastering an eager smile across her face. "Oh, no. They have me in coach but I couldn't miss the chance to say hello." She delivers me a cross-examination style glare, then shifts a more amicable one to Antonio. "You're not sitting alone today?"

He curtly replies, "Nope. This is Daniella."

I extend my hand to shake hers and she proceeds to shove her hands in her pockets.

Witch.

She tosses back her hair, saying, "Hmm. Well, enjoy the flight." She hikes back toward coach, leaving a trail of cheap perfume in her wake.

Antonio leans into me, our shoulders pressing. "Sorry about that. That woman gives me the creeps. I guess she likes me or something."

"You think?" I say, and we both laugh.

"I usually sit alone during flights to Milan. I purchase both seats to save me the headache of some oddball sitting next to me."

"Are there many oddballs in first class?"

He tilts his head. "You'd be surprised."

⚜

Hours have passed by much quicker than I expected for an eight-hour flight. Antonio and I have spent time eating, reviewing lingerie catalogs of competitors, discussing details of The Ball—all of which sound amazing.

He leans back in his seat, placing his folded hands in his lap. "Enough work stuff. Let's move on to more personal things."

I too lean back, turning my head to face him. "Personal?"

Offering a side grin, he looks at me with intent. "Yes. I think we should take time to learn more about each other, given we'll be spending nearly two weeks together."

"Okay. And how do we accomplish that? Play twenty questions or something?"

He chuckles. "How about just three. Tell me three things no one knows about you."

I could go all out and tell him at least one thing no one knows: I think I may have a crush on my new boss—despite the fact I've sworn off men and there is the *Nonna* factor.

But I think it's best to keep this one all to myself.

CHAPTER 17

ANTONIO

Daniella Belle drives me crazy.

That is, in a feel-good, I-want-you-so-bad-it-drives-me-crazy kind of a way. Nevertheless, I think I'm doing an academy-award-winning act of portraying this cool business-focused guy, who is not at all interested.

Although, I have mentally punched myself a few times when I caught myself flirting.

And staring.

The woman is, after all, absolutely mesmerizing—getting to me like no other.

Perhaps it's due to the simple fact I can't have her.

Yep. That's gotta to be it.

How the hell am I to survive ten days in Milan with this woman?

Avoid any time alone with her—at all costs.

We're almost there, maybe just a couple of hours to spare. I've had an ingenious idea of how to get to know her a little better—asking her to tell me three things about herself that no one else knows.

Her green eyes glisten as she thinks of what to share.

"Okay. I'm ready." She lets out a soft giggle. "One: Taylor

Swift is the *only* celebrity that I would have a full-on fangirl moment over, if I met her. Two: thunder and lightning frightens the hell out of me. And…" She hesitates for only a moment, then takes a deep breath. "Three: I sleep completely nude."

Wait. What? Did she just say *nude*?

As in…

Bare. Hot. Nakedness.

Someone just kill me.

The mere thought of Daniella naked makes me all—

"Nude?" I swallow the sizable lump in my throat.

"I know. TMI, right? But you did ask for three things and—"

"Why nude?" I interrupt.

"It's quite simple, actually. I can't stand the way clothes get all tangled up in the covers. So sleeping nude eliminates that problem. You should try it."

Next to you? I shake the illicit thought from my head.

"And what about you?"

"No. I don't sleep nude. Yet." A chuckle escapes me.

A wry smile surfaces. "I meant, what are your three things? That no one knows about you? Her long eyelashes fan her gorgeous face as she sits, face on palm, eager to hear my reply.

Right. This is supposed to be dual participation. *Think, Antonio.*

"Okay, Miss Belle. Three things. One: I've never seen one Godfather movie. Two: the color yellow makes be wanna barf. And three: I would give anything to live a normal guy's life."

Daniella looks at me, wonder shooting through her eyes to mine. "A normal guy's life?"

I lower my gaze from her penetrating one. "Yep. You know, no paparazzi, no semi-fame. Just a regular guy living life with no spectators."

"I see. Then you should plan your escape."

I look up now, intrigued by her suggestion. "Plan my escape?" I laugh lightly.

"Yeah. For instance, if you could go anywhere in the world, away from it all, where would you go?"

A deserted island with you. Duh. "I never actually gave much thought to that. Maybe I'd escape to a little town in Italy. Live in a modest-sized home."

"Now that you've got it all planned out, you should make it happen. Even if it's only for a week or two. Unwind. No phone. No internet. No work. Nothing but solitary freedom."

"Are you wearing your confident panties again? You're good at making convincing suggestions." I wink, and her face beams.

"I never leave home without them." She winks back, being just as coy.

She's pretty keen and I admit, this suggested plan sounds quite enticing. I could stand to get away from it all for a few days. Or for a year. Or forever—operating *CraveMe* remotely. Only, part of me is too chicken to take such a leap.

Alone, anyway.

"Why are you afraid of thunder and lightning?" I say, covertly taking our conversation back to her.

She wilts into the seat, quickly turning away, now looking out the window. "I grew up in Texas where rainstorms are pretty intense, hurricane-like, in fact."

"Okay…there's more, right?"

She shifts in her seat, facing me again, a dull grimace emerging. "Right. Well, I didn't have the luxury of curling up in Mommy and Daddy's bed during my first storm, all safe and protected. My foster mom wasn't *that* generous. Sure, my two foster sisters, her own daughters, got that. But not me. I was told there was no room for all of us and I was sent back to my room. Alone. The growling and rumbling sounds of the thunder—violently shaking my windows, echoing throughout my entire room—it was all too frightening for me, then only five years old, so I ended up sleeping in the closet. And…I've been frightened ever since."

My mouth falls open, and if I've ever had a *sorry I probed* moment, this would definitely top all others.

I imagine a young and frightened Daniella. Shame on her foster mom for being so…uncaring.

"Daniella, I totally shouldn't have intruded." I place my hand on her arm, hoping it comforts her in some way. God knows I want to hold her.

But I can't cross that line.

"It's okay. I just don't tell too many people. It's kind of embarrassing. Me all grown up now and still afraid of thunderstorms." She scoffs under her breath. "Luckily there aren't too many in Los Angeles." She smiles, a signal her slightly somber mood has eased into a more jovial one.

I'll never bring it up again. Nor will I probe into why she had a foster mom. Even though I am hungry to know what happened to her own parents.

"So back to you, now." She wriggles her way into a more comfortable position, now sitting cross-legged. "We've totally gotta get you to watch *The Godfather*. I mean it's the ultimate guy flick."

I stifle a laugh. "Is there no end to your suggestions?" Not only is this woman so incredibly foxy, she's also quite adorable.

She purposely flutters her long butterfly-like lashes. "I am the queen of suggestions."

"*Buonasera*, Ladies and Gentlemen; as we start our descent, please make sure your seat-backs and tray tables are in their full upright position. Make sure your seat belt is securely fastened and all carry-on luggage is stowed underneath the seat in front of you or in the overhead bins. *Grazie*."

The flight attendant's announcement seems to startle both Daniella and me, abruptly ending our conversation.

It's been a long flight indeed, but an enjoyable one at that, with her by my side.

And now, Milan.

With Daniella.

God help me.

MILAN, ITALY

"Elegance Is The Balance Between Proportion, Emotion, & Surprise." - Valentino Garvani

CHAPTER 18

DANIELLA

"I think I died and just woke up in heaven, you guys! Look at this room!" I flip the camera on my phone from front to back, to allow Emma and Stacy a grand view of my fabulous hotel room.

I promised them a FaceTime call as soon as I got to Milan and my timing seems perfect for them both. Stacy is working from home today, exhausted from her week-long trip to New York and Emma is off for a school holiday. It's a little after 9 a.m. in Los Angeles, while it's just after 6 p.m. here, in gorgeous Milan. It seems like it took ages for Antonio and me to exit the plane, gather our luggage, and get through customs. A driver was waiting to whisk us away via a fancy black limousine to luxurious *Bulgari Hotel Milano*. A.K.A. Heaven.

"Holy shit. It looks so damn legit!" Emma squeals.

Stacy and I both scold her about her language.

"It is quite amazing, hon," exclaims Stacy. "I bet it costs a fortune to stay there."

I flip the camera view back to my face. "I've never stayed in a place like this. I feel like a princess."

Emma giggles. "And Antonio Michaels is your prince."

"Shut up, Emma. I've sworn off men. And besides that, I believe he's got some Italian model hottie here. I overheard some of their phone conversation and he said *Ti adoro* which, I'm pretty sure, means *I adore you.*"

Both Stacy and Emma's faces seem to turn to stone, frozen with a look of shock-filled disappointment.

"Oh, well. Italian hottie or not, he looked like he was pretty into you at the airport," Stacy says through a stifled yawn.

"Wait. What?" I say, plunging onto the fluffy four-poster bed.

"Oh, you haven't seen what TMZ captured?" Emma says, disappearing from view.

"Uh, not yet. Enlighten me."

Emma comes back into view with her phone in hand. "Well, it hasn't quite made the show yet, but it's on their website." She lets out another one of her squeals as she scrolls through her phone, making me think she quite enjoys me being in the media.

Stacy clears her throat. "Brace yourself, Daniella."

"You ready?" Emma grins.

"Sure. Go for it." I adjust the pillows and prop myself upright, bracing myself for—whatever.

"Okay, so first the headline: *Enemies to Lovers? Antonio Michaels and Daniella Belle (Previously Known as Miss Potty Mouth) Arrive at LAX…Together. And We've Got the Exclusive Photos.*"

Enemies to lovers? Photos? As in more than one?

Emma holds her phone up to the screen, showing two photos of Antonio and me. The first one shows us walking side by side, stepping through the double door entrance of LAX. In it, Antonio and I are both looking at each other and smiling. And the other…a snapshot of us stepping onto the escalator, Antonio's arm clearly around my waist.

Emma emphatically points to his arm and grins. "D, you've got some serious explaining to do."

Oh. My. God.

Now I see how situations captured by overzealous paparazzi behind a lens can be thrown out of proportion. I shake my head and I don't know if I should be annoyed or flattered by the photo's inference. "You both know I tend to be a little clumsy. I tripped while stepping onto the escalator and Antonio caught me, and it appears as though that photo was captured right at the moment it occurred. It looks like I'm leaning into him and he's embracing me. But that's not at all what happened."

Both Emma and Stacy flatten their lips and raise their eyebrows. I swear they are like the same person at times.

"I'm serious!" I say, clearly defending my story.

"Well, pictures don't lie, D. He's into you. I can totally see it." Emma says, arms folded.

Stacy elbows Emma on the side. "That's enough. Go shower so we can get ready to buy some groceries."

"Bye, D," Emma says, blowing a kiss. "Send lots of photos. I'll text you later. Love ya!"

"Love ya too, babe. Behave yourself."

Stacy looks at me, her dark brown eyes speculative and knowing at the same time. "You like him. I can tell. Nothing gets by me."

It's true. Nothing tends to get by Stacy, having personally crossed-examined hundreds as a lawyer. But this time, she's dead wrong.

"I have no idea what you're talking about." I give her a frosty side-eye.

"Bullshit. When you wake up from that dream, please let me know. Anyway"—she gives a dismissive wave of her hand—"I need to get dressed. Try to live it up *princess-style* in Milan. And enjoy your time with Antonio. Stop getting caught up in that *I've sworn off men* bullshit. If it's meant to be, you can't fight it. Bye-bye, love."

Hmm. Stacy and Emma can draw whatever conclusions they want. They'll see. There will never be anything between me and Antonio.

Ever.

ANTONIO SUGGESTED I TAKE TIME TO REST UP WHILE HE TENDS TO some business obligations. So, I'll spend the rest of the evening hunkered down in my suite, immersed in the hotel room's majestic 18th Century décor and lavish amenities.

The room is at least 1,200 square feet with hardwood floors and walls painted a dark tan with burgundy and white trim. Florentine-red-colored velvet curtains cover the huge bay window that overlooks a private garden courtyard. The living room has an enormous flat-screen television, a sofa positioned near a bookshelf full of books all about Italian culture, a small oval table, and two antique side chairs. The bedroom has a king-sized poster bed as well as another huge flat-screen television. The bathroom: to die for. Not only is there a huge Roman soaking tub, but there's a walk-in shower with five shower heads. Of course, there are many spa-like lotions, soaps, and shampoos, that I will gladly take back home to Emma.

I pull back the velvety curtains and peek outside. It's dark now, but I can sense the excitement looming.

Milan.

I can't believe I'm actually here.

I would love to get out—venture about. But unfortunately, I have to rely on Antonio since I know nothing about the city. He said he'll try to take me around a little after we visit the factory tomorrow morning.

So, for now, my first night in Milan will be spent with me

taking a long bubble bath, ordering a room-service dinner, then crashing out in the comfy bed.

I close the curtains, switch off the lights in the living room, then head into the bathroom to draw a bath. I don't even wait until it's completely full before I undress and sink into the bubbles. I scoop up a mound of suds with the palm of my hand and blow, sending a flurry of bubbles into the air.

At this moment, I feel like Julia Roberts's character in Pretty Woman. Wait. So does that make Antonio, Richard Gere's character? He certainly was quite dashing in that movie.

Prince Charming-ish.

Yet, that movie had *fairy-tale ending* written all over it, and almost everyone knows that I—Daniella Belle—am a big-time Scrooge when it comes to all things fairy tale.

CHAPTER 19

DANIELLA

D espite a pesky case of jet lag, waking up in Italy fills my soul with absolute jubilation. I was even too excited to order a room service breakfast to eat.

Antonio texted me about an hour ago, reminding me that we have an appointment at the factory. Sometimes I feel our roles are reversed; shouldn't *I* be the one keeping tabs on appointments? However, in my defense, he hasn't shared the complete itinerary of this business trip. All I know is today we are to have a meeting at his uncle's factory where all of the *CraveMe* pieces are made. Beyond that I have no clue. And he did ask me to pack a small overnight bag with a change of clothes just in case he's too tired to make the drive back to Milan this evening.

It's cold outside, and I'm glad I was able to shop for this trip. Living in California does nothing to prepare residents for *real* winters.

So today's ensemble:

Designer jeans. Black boots. A long-sleeve blouse.

Hair down—parted in the middle—long and straight. Wool coat.

A quick tap at the door startles me at first, but I know it's

Antonio beckoning. He's only in the suite across the hall, after all.

I grab my purse and unlock the door, opening it to his—

I fucking swear, is there no end to how perfect this man can look?

"*Buongiorno,* sunshine. Did you sleep well?"

I'm unable to answer just yet, still thrown off-kilter by Antonio Super Hottie.

A black medium-length trench coat. Black dress slacks. Black oxfords. Muscle-hugging dress shirt.

And…hair done up in an *I Woke Up Like This* style.

I bite my lower lip and want to kick myself for suddenly becoming a mute.

For the love of all things fashion, get a hold of yourself, woman.

So I settle for a half-smile and what turns out to be an embellished nod.

"Great. Did you eat? If not, we can grab breakfast. They have good pastries and wonderful espresso."

"Breakfast sounds good, thanks." I let the door slam closed behind me, and the two of us stand in the hall, gazes fixed, until he motions for me to follow.

As we enter the restaurant, located in the lobby of the hotel, Antonio is greeted immediately by a host.

"*Signor Michaels, è un piacere rivederla.*"

"*Grazie, Leonardo, anche per me.*"

The host looks at me and nods courteously. "*Buongiorno, Signorina.*"

I smile and nod in return, hoping to God, he didn't ask me a question expecting me to provide a detailed answer.

I've so gotta pick up an English to Italian dictionary.

"She speaks English, Leonardo." Antonio smiles, placing his arm around me, sensing my discomfort, I suppose.

"Of course, *Signore.* Would you two like a table?"

"Yes, please. My usual spot."

"Of course. We reserved it, knowing you're in town.

Welcome back, by the way," Leonardo says, speaking English very fluently, albeit with a sultry Italian accent. He's a tall, older man, with heavy wrinkles defining his face. He grabs two small menus and gestures for us to follow him, leading the way past a few occupied tables to the back of the restaurant. Away from everyone else.

"Here you are," he says, pulling out a chair for me to take a seat. "And here are your menus. Can I get you both something to drink?"

"I'll have an espresso, please," Antonio says, peering down at his phone.

Leonardo nods. "And you, *Signorina*? Would you like espresso, as well?"

"May I have a latte?"

Leonardo tilts his head, shooting me a doubtful glance, and Antonio immediately lifts his gaze from his phone to me.

"Uh, *Signorina*…just to be certain, you would like a cup of milk?"

Antonio flashes an empathy-laced smile. "She'll have an espresso macchiato, Leonardo. Thank you," Antonio replies, saving me further embarrassment.

I smile appreciatively and hide behind my now-open menu.

Antonio chuckles. "You're cute. I should have warned you about the latte. But I just assumed you wanted espresso."

"And an espresso macchiato is?"

"Espresso with a splash of frothy milk. I think you'll enjoy it."

Feeling it's safe to remove the menu from shielding my rosy face, I find my voice and reply, "Thank you. I reckon while we're here, you can order for me."

"That's too much pressure. What if I order something you don't like?"

"I'll starve and lose a few pounds. Then people will mistake me for a lean and hot model."

He leans into the table, his eyes dancing around mine. "Like they don't mistake you for one, already?"

He's not flirting. He's only being polite.

Feeling a flash of heat overtake me, I pick up a folded cloth napkin and fan my face.

And this is only the *beginning* of day one in Milan.

Only nine more days to go.

Complimentary pastries are delivered to our table, along with our smooth-tasting espressos. I'm still a little too excited to eat more than a couple of bites of my cornetto—which is a light pastry similar to a croissant. And Antonio is engrossed in his phone.

"TMZ has us pegged as lovers," he says, looking annoyed.

"Right. Emma showed me the photos last night."

"Daniella, I am so sorry to have your name smeared over the media. I-I thought for sure the sunglasses would help. But I suspect they followed me from my house to yours, most likely tipped about my airline reservation." He signals for the waiter who served our food.

"I'm not concerned. I mean, I know very few people who will even care about me in the news." I reach over and touch his hand. "Seriously, it's okay."

He raises his eyebrows briefly. "Well, if you say so. Still, I want to protect your dignity in the future. I'll figure something out."

Leonardo comes and clears the table. "Thank you, *Signore*. Do you need something else?"

"No, thank you. Just the check, please."

"*Signor* Michaels…it's on the house. Enjoy the rest of your day." He nods and walks away.

"I hate when they won't let me pay." Antonio tosses his napkin onto the table. "C'mon, we need to pick up the car."

"No more fancy limo driver?"

"Nope. I like to drive myself when at all possible. They have cars to rent here, so I reserved a Maserati."

A Maserati? Why am I not at all surprised?

The valet pulls up in a white Maserati, gets out, and tosses Antonio the keys. "*La Sua auto, Signore.*"

"*Grazie, amico mio, lo apprezzo.*" Antonio walks over to the luxury car and opens the passenger door, looking straight at me. "Come on, Miss Personal Assistant. Time to head to the factory."

۞

IT'S THE WEEK BEFORE WHAT'S KNOWN AS "FASHION WEEK" AND the streets of Milan are already satiated with sartorial perfection. As Antonio maneuvers his sporty rental car through the busy intersections of Milan, I spot model-types prancing about the famous shopping district, bedecked in everything from flappy dress suits to eye-popping print dresses. There are photographers abound, feverishly snapping away at unsuspecting—and equally suspecting—passersby.

This is indeed everything I dreamed Milan would be—and more.

We finally make it to a main highway leading toward Northern Italy—a place called Bergamo—where his uncle's small factory is.

"Sit back and relax, Daniella. We've got an hour's drive ahead of us, at least," Antonio informs, looking over to me, his blue eyes much darker than normal. Besides that, I also noticed his voice sounds slightly different. More authentic.

"You're speaking with a slight Italian accent. Did you know that?"

He laughs with cheeks dusted a light coat of red, much like an embarrassed young boy. "Oh, yes. Seems as though the instant I begin speaking Italian, an accent pops up. I can't help it."

I shrug. "I suppose it's much like when I visit Texas. My Texas drawl prominently surfaces."

"Exactly. Then you can totally relate."

I steal a lengthy glance, not long enough to call it a stare, but just enough to capture him in a moment of vulnerability as he keeps his eyes on the open road—seemingly deep in thought.

My mind is saturated with a bazillion questions as I feel compelled to know more about what makes Antonio Michaels tick.

"How did you learn to speak Italian?" I say, disrupting the momentary silence.

"My grandma. She's Italian and speaks English too, but having raised me, she thought I should know Italian as well." His eyes narrow as the sun beams into the car.

"So you're Italian."

He chuckles. "Is that a statement or a question?"

"I'm sorry." I giggle. "It was meant to be a question—mainly because I get the sense it's a little more than Italian."

"Very intuitive. I'm a mutt—a mix of Italian on my mother's side and French-American on my father's side."

I knew I picked up on that mixture when we collided on the Metro.

"Very complementary mix."

"I suppose. And you?" He turns to me, his lips forming a half-smirk, half-smile that could probably charm the panties off any woman he meets.

"I'm not too sure." I begin to fidget and shift my gaze out the window. I don't particularly like speaking about anything that has to do with my family. "I've heard I have Latin roots on my mom's side, which is probably where I get my mostly tanned skin tone."

"There are many ladies who pay good money to look as naturally sun-kissed as you do, you know. It's beautiful. You're beautiful, Daniella."

I feel my entire face—well, actually—my entire body heat up.

And now what am I supposed to say?

"Thank you, Antonio," I mutter, still internally beaming.

During the rest of the drive, Antonio explains more about what we will be doing this week and also provides details about what I should expect the following week. According to him, the closer Fashion Week approaches, the crazier it will get.

He exits the highway and we take some side streets until he turns onto a street called *Via Confortino*. And then we pull into a parking lot in front of a small factory.

"And here we are: my uncle's factory."

The two of us are out of the car for only thirty seconds when a tall, thin man with dark hair and a well-trimmed salt-and-pepper-colored beard approaches, arms spread out, headed right for Antonio. *"Benvenuto, nipote mio!"* He cups Antonio's face in his large hands, planting a kiss on one cheek, then the other.

"Hello, Uncle Carlo. It's great to see you," Antonio says, switching the conversation from Italian to English, for my benefit, I assume.

His uncle looks at me with widened eyes and raised eyebrows. "Ooooh. Such a beauty. Is this a girlfriend you've been hiding, eh, *bel diavoletto?*"

Antonio seems to swallow his embarrassment and clears his throat. "Uncle Carlo, this is Daniella Belle. My new assistant."

"'Your assistant? *E' così che si chiama adesso?*"

Antonio rolls his eyes. "No, Uncle. Assistant still means assistant. Not a new term for girlfriend."

Uncle Carlo approaches and greets me in the same manner he did Antonio, planting a kiss on one of my cheeks before moving to the other. "It's good to meet you, Daniella Belle. And welcome to Italy."

He stands between me and Antonio and claps his hands. "Shall we go on in? We have lots of work to do, I hear."

He leads the way through the factory doors, taking us past endless rows of floor-to-ceiling shelving filled with layers of color-categorized garment fabric.

We end up in an office, its walls splattered with labeled sketches of all sorts of designs—from coats, to pants, to shoes, dresses, and lingerie.

He encourages me to sit on a small white sofa, perched against a copper-toned wall displaying vibrant artwork of small Italian cities. I sit down, sinking into the couch cushions, feeling a little tired now. Jet lag to blame, no doubt.

Uncle Carlo sits on the edge of his desk and opens a drawer, pulling out a pack of cigarettes and a lighter. "Mind if I smoke?"

Antonio shakes his head. "Uncle Carlo...put those away. Does Aunt Bettina know you're smoking again?"

Uncle Carlo grimaces, placing the pack of cigarettes and lighter back in the desk drawer. "No. And you better not tell her." He smiles. "I'm doing much better now anyway, only down to one or two cigarettes a week." He coughs and grabs a bottle of water and takes a gulp. "Oh, can I offer you both something to drink?"

I shake my head and both Antonio and I offer a, "No thank you," in harmonious unison.

Uncle Carlo laughs. "Hmm. Soon you two will be completing each other's sentences." He professes, his thick Italian accent brimming.

What is that supposed to mean?

"So, Uncle, let's discuss the designs. Do you have the sketches?"

"Yes, of course." Uncle Carlo removes a black portfolio from the top of his desk and hands it over to Antonio.

"Great. I just need to tweak these a bit, then get them back to you tomorrow morning."

"Not big tweaks, I hope?"

"No. Very subtle, but necessary. Anyway, we need to look at fabric that is…less sheer."

"Certainly. Follow me."

Antonio and I spend the next couple of hours perusing all sorts of fabric from sheer lace to sheer chiffon, along with numerous types of silk, then rayon, spandex, nylon, cotton, and even some knit fabric. We then create a book full of swatches of fabrics we like best, in addition to swatches of colors we think befits the style we wish to emulate. And all the while I am beaming inside, gratified Antonio is affording me the opportunity to assist with picking out fabrics and colors on a project so grandiose.

Soon after, we pack up and head out, promising to return early the next morning.

"See you here bright and early then. *A domani.*" Uncle Carlo waves as we drive off.

"Thanks for your help, Daniella. Your design training has proved most significant. I'm really happy you accepted the job." Antonio looks at me and smiles.

I offer a smile in return when his phone rings, and he instantly answers, "*Sì, Nonna. Sto guidando, ci vediamo presto.*" He ends the short call, with a satisfying glow on his face.

A *Nonna* glow. Ugh.

"Are you hungry?" he asks, and I hope the disgust I feel hearing him talk all, presumably, lovey-dovey has not surfaced to my face.

"Yes, I am actually." I only nibbled on a small portion of the pastry this morning and I feel as though my blood sugar has dropped.

"Great, so am I. We'll eat soon. Nonna has prepared a feast for us."

Wait. *Nonna*? Prepared a feast for…*us*?

I turn to face him, my mouth slightly ajar even before words are ready to fly out. "I'm sorry? You're taking me to

Nonna's house? Are you sure that's a good idea? I mean, isn't there a drive thru—a Burger King or something?"

"Burger King? You're in Italy and you want me to take you to eat a burger and fries?" He lets out a hard chuckle. "You're a riot, Daniella Belle."

Riot or not, I don't think I'm prepared to meet this *Nonna* hot model chick. I mean things could get awkward.

I smile wryly. "She doesn't mind you bringing me along?"

"Not at all. She's looking forward to meeting you, in fact. I hardly bring anyone with me when I visit her. She welcomes the extra company. The more, the merrier."

The more, the merrier? Eww. I'm sure my face has turned pale by now.

"Relax, Daniella. I promise you'll have a great time getting to know Nonna. And I'm sure we will spend the night there as well, especially since we've gotta get back to the factory in the morning. Besides, Nonna expects me to spend the night whenever I'm in town. It gives us time to catch up."

Hmm. I bet.

I plaster on the widest smile possible. "Sounds wonderful. I look forward to meeting her."

I fold my arms in protest, but I don't think Antonio notices my objection.

Minutes later, Antonio turns onto a small street filled with rows of quaint homes. He pulls into the driveway of a blue house with an orange roof.

This looks nothing like a home of an Italian model. I expected something less country and more palatial.

"Ready?" asks an eager Antonio.

"About as ready as I'll ever be."

I exit the car and prepare myself for what's next: the moment I come face-to-face with the woman who seems to make Antonio light up at the mere sight of her name and sound of her voice.

CHAPTER 20

ANTONIO

T his may sound crazy, but I'm a nervous wreck about introducing Daniella to Nonna, being that Nonna means so much to me.

I value her opinion more than anyone else's.

Yet it's funny, Daniella looks more nervous than I am right now. Or maybe it's just pure hunger, having barely touched any of the pastries this morning. As expected, she looks hotter than ever. Tight-fitting jeans—and I unashamedly caught myself admiring how they perfectly caress her rump—along with a plunging neckline top, which leaves a tasteful amount of cleavage visible to my hungry-for-her eyes.

Thank goodness I'll be busy with Fashion Show and Lingerie Ball planning activities. If I didn't have those to distract me for the next several days, I don't think I'd be able to stand being around her so long without the two of us—

"So this is Nonna's place, huh?" Daniella asks, putting an end to my internal meltdown.

"Yep. I've tried to get her to move to a more metropolitan area, but she loves this house. And actually, I do too. It's country-like, faraway from those spectators I try so hard to stay hidden from," I explain as the two of us walk up the cobblestone steps leading to the front door.

She nods, arms folded, still looking incredibly beside herself.

"You okay? You look—"

"Yes," she interjects, "I think I'm just hungry. And tired."

"Well, Nonna is a remarkable cook and will certainly make sure you get your fill. It's the Italian in her."

As we approach the front door, I feel my heart beat out of my chest.

Get a hold of yourself, man—they are going to hit it off.

"Nonna?" I shout out, after opening the door. "I told you to keep the door locked."

Women. Sometimes they never listen.

I help Daniella out of her coat and hang it on the hook by the door alongside mine. "She never locks the door in the daytime. I wish she'd listen to me—stubborn as most Italian women."

Daniella nods and I can tell she's surveying the house. It's quaint and completely old-fashioned—and all Nonna.

I grab Daniella's hand and lead her to the kitchen. "I've gotta admit. I'm nervous and don't know why. Maybe it's because this is a first for me. Introducing someone—a woman —to Nonna."

Daniella frowns. "And why is that?"

"Because no one has been—"

"Antonio? Is that you? *Mi sembrava di aver sentito il mio nipote preferito.*"

"Yes, it's me. And, of course, I'm your favorite. I am, after all, your *only* grandson."

The clip-clop of shoes pound the tile floor, then Nonna appears from the kitchen, a wooden spoon in her hand, and she immediately embraces me.

Daniella's eyes widen and a smile consumes her entire face. "Did you say, grandson? Nonna is your *grandmother*?"

I pull away from my seventy-five-year-old grandma and chuckle. "Of course, she's my grandmother. Anyway, Nonna this is Daniella and Daniella, this is Nonna—which in Italian means Grandma."

Daniella beams with delight as she pulls Nonna close and gives her a warm hug. "Oh, Nonna, you have *no* idea how happy I am to meet you."

Nonna pulls back, rubbing her hands along the side of Daniella's arms, giving her a sizable once-over. She's much shorter than Daniella is in her high-heeled boots. "*Signorina*, it's a pleasure to meet you." She turns her head to face me. "You're right, *nipote*. She's quite stunning."

I look away, embarrassed. Perhaps I should have warned Nonna to be more discreet about the way I feel about Daniella.

Laughing nervously, I come up with something to say, to change the subject. "We're starving, Nonna."

"*Oh, sì, venite a mangiare,*" she says, then looks back to Daniella. "Let's eat!"

We gather in the kitchen, sitting around the table that's been covered in the same blue-and-white floral tablecloth for years. Nonna serves up a few of my favorite dishes that always make me think of home—Saltimbocca - veal wrapped in prosciutto, Lasagne, and Osso Buco alla Milanese - another veal dish braised in vegetables and white wine. *Perfetto*.

The three of us talk freely about Italy, the impending fashion show, and the *CraveMe* business, as we all pig out, Daniella seeming to equally enjoy the feast. I listen to the two of them chatting non-stop, as if they were long lost friends who never missed a beat.

AFTER WE EAT ALL THAT WE POSSIBLY CAN, THE THREE OF US TIDY up and retire to the living room, too full to move. Nonna tells us both there is homemade gelato in the freezer, should we develop a sweet tooth later. And by the time nightfall surfaces, Daniella's yawns tell me it's time to show her to her room.

"I hope you don't mind sleeping here tonight. I just don't wish to battle the drive and the Milan traffic."

"Oh, I don't mind at all. I'm glad you told me about the overnight bag. I've got everything I need for the night." She yawns as she walks alongside me down the narrow hallway to the guest room.

We reach the end of the hall and I slowly open the guest room door, wishing I didn't have to say goodnight just yet. But I know she's tired and we have another early day tomorrow. "Here's your room. I'm sure Nonna has fixed it up nice for you. She likes company, that's for sure—and I can tell she especially likes you."

Through sleepy eyes, Daniella's gaze dances with mine. "Thanks for today, Antonio. I feel honored to have been introduced to Nonna. She's a special lady and I can see why you light up whenever you speak with her."

"I do?"

"Mmm-hmmm." She bites down on her lower lip. "Can I share something?"

I lean into the door frame, arms folded. "Of course."

She stares to the ceiling, seeming to search for the right words to say. "Each time you spoke with Nonna on the phone, I thought she was some Italian hottie model you meet up with whenever you're in Milan." She breathes in and out. Then meets my gaze again.

I let out an amused chuckle. "I see. Is that what was bothering you earlier? You thought I was going to introduce you to my Italian hottie lover?"

She nods vigorously, with her index finger over her pressed lips.

I lean in closer to her and softly whisper, "Daniella Belle, I have no Italian lover and in fact, according to TMZ, *you* are my lover, remember?"

And with that we break out into laughter, before I bid her a very good night.

CHAPTER 21

DANIELLA

The starlit sky creeps through the open window shade as I sluggishly awaken from, what seems like hours of sleep.

A smile looms on my face upon my reflection of the last encounter I had with Antonio before I slid out of my clothes, showered, and eased into this small, yet cozy twin-sized bed.

He's amusing, warmhearted, sexy, and…charming.

And Nonna is everything I imagined a loving grandmother to be with her grayish hair, black-rimmed eyeglasses, and warm smile. I have been trying to dismiss the fact that I assumed she was his Italian hottie. That'll teach me to ever make irrational judgments again. Watching the way Antonio looks up to her made me all warm and fuzzy inside, immediately causing me to think that as soon as I'm over this swearing-off-men phase, finding a man like him will be the top of my wish list.

The digital clock on the dresser blinks continuously—evidently it hasn't been programmed in quite some time.

I pick up my phone to check the time, certain I've already slept most of the night away. By the time I got out of the shower and dried off, I practically crawled into bed.

But shit.

It's only 11 p.m., meaning I've slept for a whopping three hours.

So, now what?

It's not like I can just turn over and instantly fall back to sleep.

This jet lag thing is pretty fucked up.

Maybe Antonio is awake, too.

After debating in my head whether I should send him a text or not, I finally decide to go for it.

Me: Hi. Are you awake? I can't seem to fall back to sleep.

Antonio: In the dining room working and eating gelato. Why don't you join me? I can use some feedback on these sketch revisions.

I think for at least two minutes before I reply.

Me: Okay. I'm on my way.

Peeling back the covers, the cold air hits my bare skin, causing goose bumps to surface all over my naked body. Perhaps I'll have to rethink this sleeping in the nude thing while I'm in this much colder climate.

Leaping out of bed, I dart into the bathroom, finding sweatpants, a T-shirt, and a cardigan sweater in my overnight bag. Shivering, I slip into them before making my way out to the dining room.

Antonio sits, shirt partially unbuttoned, hair slightly awry, and he's wearing eyeglasses. He looks like a young hot professor that every girl in the class has a secret crush on.

I slide into the chair across from his. "Hi."

He looks up from his tablet, startled. "Hey. I didn't even hear you come in." He removes his glasses. "Would you like some gelato? It's really good."

"Gelato? I'm freezing! Plus, I doubt a cold dessert will help me sleep."

He laughs. "I doubt it too. How about some chamomile tea then? That should help you fall asleep. And I'll turn on the heater. I hadn't really noticed just how cold it is in here."

"Thanks. And I'd love some tea. Where is it?"

"Oh no, allow me. Why don't you come sit down here and take a look at these designs? Tell me what you think." He stands, gesturing for me to sit in his chair, then disappears into the kitchen to make my tea while I peruse the designs.

He's got skills, that's for sure. Endless lines of exquisite detail. No wonder his lingerie sells the volume it does.

He returns, hot cup of tea in hand. "Here you go." While easing into the seat next to mine, he sets the cup on the table. "So, what do you think? Feedback, please."

"They're absolutely beautiful. And I can tell they'll be far less sheer in places that matter. What about adding some color trim to a few of the panties, to allow for mixing and matching the bra with panties?" I suggest, holding back the desire to just comfort him by rubbing my fingers through his perfectly messy hair. Poor guy looks mentally exhausted.

In a hot way, of course.

"I like that idea. I'll add some before I go to bed." He pushes the tablet to the side. "We need to discuss a few intricacies regarding the show as well as the ball."

I take a sip of tea. "Okay. I'm all ears."

Antonio winks and, for a split second, I think he wants to say something sarcastic. "Fabulous. Now when we head back to Milan tomorrow, I'm gonna need you to work on the following items." He opens up a notebook and rips out a sheet of paper containing a list of items.

1. '80s music tracks for fashion show — enough to fill our thirty-minute block

2. Runway style sets — these must match the lingerie theme/music each model will walk to

3. Runway backdrop design — what do you have in mind?

Looking up from the list, I catch him staring at me. Not a creepy kind of a stare, thank goodness.

"Anything else?"

He shifts in his seat, placing both elbows onto the table. "Uh, yes. Let's see. About the fashion show. Ramon has worked behind the scenes of each of the *CraveMe* shows, for the last five years at least, making sure all ten models are dressed and in place. You'll work with him on number two on that list. But he's in Aspen right now and isn't due to arrive here until Saturday."

I nod and continue to sip my tea.

"Right. Then," he hesitates before going on, "well, there is the issue of the ball. I uh…don't exactly have a date this year."

I feel my entire body heat up; maybe it's the tea or maybe it's the sudden…

"So, will you be my date this year? I promise to be a complete gentleman."

…the sudden anticipation of him asking me to be his date.

Looking at me, I'm sure it's hard to tell I'm melting inside. But I need to play it cool, not only to fool him, but to keep myself in check. I've sworn off men, and there is no way I plan on getting romantically involved with my dreamy-as-fuck boss.

This is all work-related.

Risky business.

I mean strictly business.

"Of course. Whatever you need me to do to make this event a success for *CraveMe*."

"I'm glad you feel that way. Thank you. There is one more thing."

I raise my eyebrows.

"The top lingerie designers save their newest chemise or nightgown, sporting it much like one would a custom ball gown for the ball instead of on the catwalk. And this year I am one of the top designers listed. It's a first for me and I hadn't thought of who I wanted to wear that piece, until recently."

I lift the cup to my mouth, waiting to hear more. Like, will I get to meet a famous model now and get to help dress her for the ball?

I take a sip of the, now lukewarm, tea and before I can even swallow, Antonio says, "You. I'd really like you to wear the piece I plan to feature at the ball."

Tea goes *everywhere*—sprayed out of my mouth in shock. "Shit. I'm so sorry, Antonio."

He flies up and out of his seat then begins to laugh. "Well, I wasn't expecting *that* reaction."

I spring up from the chair, dash into the kitchen to grab a towel, then back into the dining room to clean up the tea that's splattered all over Antonio and the table. Only when I return to the dining room, I nearly pass out, coming face-to-naked-bare-pectorals. Antonio has removed his shirt and is using it to wipe up the tea off of the table.

Damn, he's like a fucking machine. I can hardly look away.

"I-I'm," I stammer, "so sorry about your shirt."

"No worries. I've got plenty."

We both sit back down and try hard to stifle our chuckles.

And I try hard to breathe like a normal person again.

"I'd be honored to wear anything *CraveMe* designed. May I see it first? Before I agree? I mean, I hope that's okay."

Antonio nods. "Certainly. It's at the factory. You'll see it tomorrow."

"Perfect, and thank you."

A corner of his mouth lifts. "For what?"

"For thinking of me. I'm flattered."

"Daniella Belle, you're a delight. But it's getting late. Go back to bed, I insist. We have a long day tomorrow."

I ease up from the chair and place my hand on his shoulder. "Good-night, Antonio."

"Until tomorrow, Daniella. Sleep well."

CHAPTER 22

DANIELLA

The next morning I wake up to the sound of a rooster's crow and the bright sun beaming down on my face, both forcing me to get up and dressed. I scurry over to the kitchen to find Nonna sitting, reading the local newspaper and munching on a fetta biscottata.

"Good morning, Nonna."

She peers up through her dark-rimmed eyeglasses and smiles brightly. "Eh! Good morning, Daniella. You sleep well?" she asks, through a heavy Italian accent.

"Yes, thank you." I sit down beside her at the table.

"Are you hungry?"

"Sort of. May I have a biscottate?" I ask, unsure if I've even pronounced it right.

"Oh, of course. What about espresso, my dear? That too?"

I nod graciously.

Minutes later, she produces the hot espresso along with the biscuit.

"Antonio. He left for the factory. He didn't want to wake you. But he said he'll return soon and you two will head back to Milan." She pats the back of my hand, seeming to try to ease any discomfort I may be feeling.

Truth is, I wasn't planning to be left behind. But it was thoughtful of him to let me sleep.

I smile. "Oh, it's fine. I don't mind hanging out here with you, Nonna."

"You have a lovely smile, Daniella." She tilts her head to the side, giving me a serious expression. "You seem to have this, uh, aura about you that comes from within. Natural. Not forced." She looks down at her biscuit. "Very similar to my Antonietta."

"I'm sorry…who?"

"Antonietta. My daughter. Antonio's mother." She smiles at the thought.

"Oh, I see. I didn't know her name. I've only seen a photograph of her."

"Oh, yes. The one when she was pregnant with Antonio, no?"

I nod.

"Did Antonio share what happened?" She looks at me, eyebrows raised.

I shake my head as I sip my espresso.

"He doesn't speak about it much since he never met her."

Nonna folds the newspaper and sits back in her chair with her arms folded over her chest as if to provide self-comfort. "Antonio's mom was a young woman of eighteen years, living here, in this very house, when she met this French-American businessman while she was shopping in Milan. My goodness, was she captivated by him. He was about ten years older than she was and had money to woo her to the moon and back. I warned her to stay away from him—that he was probably after one thing. But I couldn't deny, my daughter was a beauty with this magnetic aura." She smiles and pats my hand again. "The same aura I see in you." She sips on her espresso. "Anyway, Antonietta fell for this man and ended up following him to America—California to be exact. They had an affair for months, while he was doing business and living it up at a fancy hotel in Beverly Hills. Antonietta got a job as a housekeeper, working for this older woman who lived alone in this elaborate home in Beverly Hills. My daughter was on top of the world. Until her man, Hugo Michaels, just up and disappeared. A few months later, she realized she was pregnant."

I sit back in the chair, completely engrossed by her story. And already my heart aches for Nonna.

"I begged her to come back to Italy. Have the baby here and I'd help her raise it. But she refused, saying she loved America and was planning to stay and make it work. It broke my heart, but she was a grown woman living her life."

I finish my espresso and listen intently.

"Then, I got a phone call from Miss Tilly. Her employer. She said that my Antonietta had gone into early labor, with an elevated blood pressure. She passed away during the delivery, never having the chance to see or hold her baby boy. I was a hysterical mess. Miss Tilly flew me to Los Angeles and, when I arrived, together we came up with a plan. First, we named him Antonio, after his mom and gave him the last name of his father, the dirt bag who left my beautiful daughter. Anyway, Tilly explained how much Antonietta wanted to raise Antonio in America. So she offered to allow me to stay at her house and work part-time as a housekeeper while I raised my grandson. I agreed to do so; after losing my own husband many years before, I was alone in Italy anyway."

I nod in absolute amazement.

"So, after my daughter's funeral, I contacted my brother Carlo and explained what had happened and asked him to keep an eye on this house until I returned. So he moved in, bless his heart, and renovated it over the years while I remained in Beverly Hills raising Antonio. Miss Tilly was taken by Antonio, especially since she had no children of her own. All she had was her beautiful home and what seemed like an endless amount of money. She made sure Antonio went to the finest private schools, hired tutors for subjects he needed extra help in, and spoiled him rotten. She actually treated us both very well. And since she was much older than I was, she eventually passed away when Antonio was sixteen. She left him the house, her money, everything."

I sit wide-eyed, completely shocked. "Is that the house he lives in today?"

She nods.

"Wow. That's amazing."

"Yes. Anyway, when Antonio turned eighteen I wanted to go back to Italy. I had only been back once or twice since I left, and I missed it. I missed my house—this house." She looks around the kitchen and smiles. "Antonio wired a large amount of money into my account, saying he could never repay me for what I did for him. And soon after, I left America and came back here."

The two of us sit in silence, both taking in what had been shared. I have a newfound respect for both Antonio and Nonna, and now understand why their bond is so deep.

"Antonio started *CraveMe* when he was only nineteen years old, determined to make his way without using the money Miss Tilly left him. Aside from donating money every month to the hospital he was born at, I'm not at all certain what he plans to do with all of her money."

Nonna rises from her seat and begins to remove, our now, empty plates from the table.

"I'm not sure Antonio wanted me to share all of that with you, but I feel like I can trust you. And I can tell he likes you."

"He does?" I ask surprised, as I begin to help her set the plates and espresso cups into the kitchen sink.

"Oh, please, he'd be a fool not to. And I know my grandson. He's never brought a woman to meet me, and he's been talking about you non-stop."

I smirk at the warm feeling brewing inside of me.

Truth is, I think I like him too.

CHAPTER 23
ANTONIO

I was feeling restless, so I took off early for the factory so Daniella and I can get back to Milan sooner than planned. I know she probably looked forward to going back to the factory with me, but when I peeked in her room this morning she was sound asleep—one inviting bare leg taunting me from outside of the covers. I could only imagine how the rest of her body looked under there, remembering she told me she sleeps naked.

If she were mine I would have been naked under those covers with her.

All over her.

Touching her.

Loving every tender inch of her.

I digress…

I let Nonna know I'd be back and asked her to keep Daniella entertained while I was gone. And while at the factory, Uncle Carlo and I went over details of the changes I wanted made to the fabric and designs, and I also picked up what I hope Daniella will wear to the ball.

Uncle Carlo promised a quick turnaround, driving preliminary samples to Milan no later than Friday.

And now I'm back at Nonna's saying my farewells, leaving her tickets to the fashion show. She hugs me and whispers, "I hope you don't mind—I told Daniella all about your mother, father, and Miss Tilly."

I pull back, a little shocked—but also relieved. Better she explained all of that than I, especially since I dislike talking about any of it. "I don't mind, Nonna." I kiss her on both cheeks. "So, what do you think of her?"

"I don't think I would have shared any details about your life if I didn't like her. She's a great girl with a beautiful heart. I can see why you're so taken. But somewhere along the line, she's been hurt; I can see that in her eyes. Women who have a heavy heart tend to be very reserved. Keep that in mind, okay?"

I nod, appreciating her insight. Nonna knows her stuff and I trust her with everything.

Daniella appears from the hallway, carrying her overnight bag and boots. She's stunning as usual in a formfitting dress, matching tights, and for the first time, flat shoes, showcasing her petite height.

I immediately take her bag and boots.

"Nonna, it's been a pleasure," she says. "I'll be sure to visit again, if Antonio says it's okay."

"You're welcome anytime, with or without Antonio." She winks and the two of them embrace.

Nonna stands outside as we pull onto the road, headed back to Milan.

Buzzing in and out of traffic, I think about what Nonna said about Daniella, and I haven't stopped wondering who may have hurt her. I know it's more than the idiot who broke up with her via text. But what? Her foster parents? A love gone totally awry? I want to ask, but I don't want to push her further away. It's bad enough there is this very visible wedge between us known as *work*. I dare not create another needless wedge.

She sits quiet, peering out the window, seeming to be deep in thought. There is a mysterious intrigue about her. What makes her who she is? I hope to be fortunate enough to uncover that soon.

I decide to steal the silence. "Uncle Carlo promised a quick turnaround and will drive some samples to Milan no later than Friday."

She looks away from the window, now studying me. "That's good. I can't wait to see them."

"You okay?"

She nods. "Uh-huh. I think I'm just still getting over the excitement of being in Italy. I love it here, Antonio."

"It is a wonderful place. And part of the reason I have the factory here. I can visit whenever possible. That and to keep an eye on Nonna. I worry about her all alone."

"She's amazing, Antonio, and I can tell she's very proud of you. Your drive and your independence."

"That makes me feel good. I owe Nonna a lot for giving up eighteen years of her life in Italy to raise me in America. I'll never be able to repay her."

"Oh, but don't you see you have? The way you turned out has made it all worthwhile."

I could just pull the car over and kiss this woman right here and now.

But I won't.

"Thanks for that, Daniella. You know, for an assistant, you're pretty all right," I joke.

"I told you a couple of times already, I'm your girl."

And I so very much want to be your guy.

CHAPTER 24

DANIELLA

Ever since I was young, I killed time by sketching designs in sketchbooks that I would buy with money I earned from doing chores, sweeping hair up at the local hair salon, babysitting, or by helping the older lady across the street carry groceries in.

I had sketchbooks galore, with designs categorized by my creatively named collections.

I dreamed of being a fashion designer with top models fighting to pose in my clothes, featured in top fashion magazines like *Marie Claire*, *Harpers Bazaar*, *InStyle*, *Cosmopolitan*, and *Vogue*.

And then, when I was seventeen, I discovered a reality show—Project Runway—in which fashion contestants compete to design a collection for New York Fashion Week.

I was inspired by the rush they seemed to have, involved in all that encompassed Fashion Week. I was lucky enough to get a taste of this during my design school days.

But nothing of this magnitude.

It's been a crazy stack of days since Antonio and I returned to Milan. We both have busied ourselves deep in the throes of making sure we have everything perfectly laid out for the show—including the song set for the runway.

1. *Donna Summer—She Works Hard For The Money*

2. *Cyndi Lauper—Girls Just Wanna Have Fun*

3. *Eurythmics—Sweet Dreams*

4. *Janet Jackson—Control*

5. *Pat Benetar—Love is a Battlefield*

6. *Vanity 6—Nasty Girl*

7. *Salt-N-Pepa—Push It*

8. *Sheila E—Glamorous Life*

9. *Gloria Estefan—Conga*

10. *Madonna—Express Yourself*

Every song represents the theme and I've been working hard, sketching what I believe will best accompany lingerie pieces inspired by each song.

Purses. Shoes. Hairstyles. Hats. Jewelry. Layers of clothing —the tedious, behind-the-scenes stuff that drives designers mad.

Antonio approved of the song choices, and he was highly impressed by the sketches, believing all will beautify the scenes we present.

Now, I've gotta go hunt for many of these items, which should be a snap since I'm surrounded by every fashionable boutique I could dream of.

Only one problem: Antonio won't allow me to venture out on my own—a battle we've been *discussing* now, for over an hour.

"I don't get why you don't approve of me going on my own. You're busy with business stuff, and I should take this time to purchase all of the items on my list." I slouch down onto the sofa in the fashion expo office, arms and legs crossed in protest.

"And I don't get why you don't understand that I don't want you out on the streets of Milan on your own."

"Antonio. It's *Milan*. During Fashion Week. What could go wrong?"

He scoffs from behind the desk he's sitting at, while working on business spreadsheets. "It's not quite Fashion Week yet. And the fact that there are so many people out there right now—drawn here specifically for the event—just about *anything* could go wrong."

I roll my eyes and throw my arms in the air.

"Look, Liza and Jonah will be here Friday. I'll feel better if you go with one, or even both of them, okay?" He smiles and that, on its own, settles my grievance.

"That's two days away. What do I busy myself with until then?"

"Well." He removes something from his briefcase, stands away from his desk chair, and walks over to sit next to me. "How about you attend some of these? I won't be able to go, but I'd appreciate if my Sassy Assistant goes in my place."

"Sassy Assistant?" I mock, taking the pre-fashion-show guest pass and brochure from his hand.

"Since day one." He winks. "This pass will get you into all of the events located in this expo center and should keep you busy until Friday. I'll expect updates on all of the latest trends on fabrics and accessories."

I gesture a hand salute. "Yes, Sir."

He chuckles. "But first, how about an early dinner before the crowds take up all the restaurant space? I think we both can use a fashion-focused break."

"Pizza?"

"You've read my mind."

Pizza AM is located in Downtown Milan, with festive décor and a small menu. At first, I'm put off by their small menu options, but Antonio swears a smaller menu translates into better, more thoughtfully prepared cuisine. He takes the liberty of ordering for us. I don't want to take the chance of ordering pepperoni and get told pepperoni in Italy is actually sweet bell peppers.

"Trust me on this one."

"You're the boss," I say in a brat-ish, unfazed tone.

"Says the Sassy Assistant."

I shake my head.

I do trust him.

More than he knows.

"Thanks for the pass. I'm looking forward to attending all of the events."

"Oh, not a problem. I hope you understand my concerns. You're a beautiful woman. It's bad enough guys gawk even when you're with me."

I feel my eyebrows snap together. "No, they don't."

He snarls. "Uh, yeah, they do."

"Well, I probably haven't noticed because I've sworn off men."

His jaw drops. "You've sworn off men?"

"Yep. Ever since Jacob Ryan broke up with me via text. That day, I decided men are off limits."

His expression softens. "Interesting. And for how long?"

"How long, what?"

"Will you be men-less? A day, month, year—"

I raise my chin. "Forever."

"That's a mighty long time. You'll break a lot of hearts." He drums the tips of his fingers along the table.

"Which is so much better than anyone breaking mine."

CHAPTER 25

ANTONIO

I've kept my distance from Daniella for the last couple of days, as I stay focused on things that need to get done before the show. I'm glad she's agreed to go to pre-show events in my place and gave up on going out shopping alone in Milan.

I know how men are, and I don't want anyone trying to woo his way into her life.

Maybe I'm just wary of such instances since it's how my mother and father met. Sometimes men seek out young, beautiful women and don't care about breaking their hearts.

Although I guess I don't have to worry about anyone breaking Daniella's heart; she's 'sworn off men'.

I still shake my head at that statement.

Because *I* want her.

It's Friday and Liza and Jonah are due to arrive this evening.

Uncle Carlo has dropped off the samples and will need to make only a few tweaks before he brings the finished pieces here on Sunday—two days before the show.

There are only a few pending items left on the list, all of

which, I hope, will make it to the completion list within the next few days.

1. *Accessories and clothing needed for the walk—Daniella is to take care of this with Liza this weekend and purchase items based on her sketches. The woman has amazing talent and I trust her with this project immensely.*

2. *Make contact with Ramon, my set director—he has called me four times and each time I miss the call. When I call or text him, I get no reply in return, which concerns me. Perhaps his cell reception is poor on the ski slopes in Aspen.*

3. *Confirm Daniella will wear the showcase piece at the ball—she has it and was to try it on and let me know if she's up to wearing it. That piece will look stunning on her—as if it were made especially for her.*

Maybe I should just ask her again now, via text? It could be she doesn't want to wear it, and is too afraid to tell me in person.

Me: **Hey. How are the events going? Are you taking notes, Miss Personal Assistant?**

In all honesty, I feel odd calling her my assistant, not only because I secretly have the hots for her, but also because she's done far more than I expect an assistant to do. Sure, Dottie was excellent, but she lacked the fashion expertise and passion I see in Daniella.

Daniella: **Hey, boss. Yep. Taking copious notes like a good girl.**

Her bite still drives me crazy.

Me: **Good! So I have a question.**

Daniella: **Then why didn't you just text the question, instead of texting 'so I have a question'?**

And it seems there is no end to her sassiness.

Me: **Are you going to indulge me and wear the showcase piece to the ball?**

At least a minute has passed…and no reply. Maybe I freaked her out. I mean, she's even my date—

Oh wait. She's replied.

Daniella: **Yes. I'm so gonna rock the hell out of that shit.**

Item #3 officially crossed over to completion status.

Me: **Great! Don't forget we need to head to the airport in a couple of hours to pick up Liza and Jonah.**

Daniella: **Yep. I'm on it, boss. I'll meet you in the expo lobby.**

⚜

A FEW HOURS LATER, JONAH AND I LOAD THE SUITCASES INTO THE trunk of the car at the arrivals terminal at the airport, while Liza and Daniella have both settled in the back seat, chatting-it-up girl-style.

Jonah looks at me before I close the trunk. "So, how's your week been?"

I chuckle because I know he's referring to my time with Daniella. He knows I'm crazy about her. "It's been good. But believe me, we are still very much on Boss and Assistant grounds. And I get the feeling it's going to stay like that."

"Oh, my friend, don't give up hope. Milan is the place where you and I find our true loves…. I told you, I'm not leaving here this week without meeting the woman I'm gonna marry. You watch."

I shake my head, and close the trunk, and soon we are all on the road, headed to the hotel. But not before Liza and Jonah fall fast asleep, both impacted already by jet lag.

My phone rings and I see via caller ID it's Ramon.

Thank goodness.

"Hey, Ramon! We've been playing phone tag. How's it going? Are you headed to the airport?"

"Antonio, I've had an accident on the slope." He stammers a bit.

Crap no.

"What? What kind of an accident? Are you all right?" I can feel my heart pounding out of my chest.

"Actually, I'm not. I mean I'm alive and all, but my leg isn't so well." His voice sounds rugged as if he hasn't slept for a couple of days.

"What happened?"

"I was going down this smooth slope and somehow my skis went over a tree stump. I don't know, man...all I remember is falling and rolling and flipping, and then I woke up in the fucking hospital. I broke my right leg and my left elbow is shattered. I'm still in the hospital."

"My God, Ramon. I'm so sorry to hear that! But thank goodness nothing worse happened."

"Yeah. Well I'm not gonna make the fashion show. I can't even go home to Venice yet. I'm so sorry. I-I know how much this year means to you."

"No worries, Ramon. Is there anything I can do to help? You need anything?" I ask, I mean he's been on my team for years now, I want to help anyway that I can.

"That's just like you, man, always caring about others. You've got a show to worry about. Don't worry about me... I'll be fine."

"Okay, then. Rest up. I'll call to check on you next week. And I'll send you a video file of how the show turns out."

"Thanks, boss. Take care."

I'm screwed.

It takes ages to develop a rapport with someone enough that they live, breathe, and create your expectations on the runway. And it's not like I can just Google one and—boom— I'll find one. Now. During Fashion Week.

Damn it. I slam my fist against the steering wheel.

"You okay?" mutters Daniella from the back seat.

"Not really. But I don't want to discuss it right now," I snap.

And I don't. Why should I pull her in? She can't have

anything to offer anyway. Unless she knows someone I can call to help.

"Oh, I see," she says with an abrasive tone.

And great. I probably hurt her feelings now, or something. I promised I wouldn't be a dick when I'm upset. And looks like I did it again.

We arrive at the hotel and Jonah and Liza both wake up, surprised and embarrassed they fell asleep in the car.

And just as soon as the valet removes their bags, they are assisted by the hotel manager to check in and get settled.

Daniella and Liza arrange a time to meet to shop for items needed for the show, then Daniella and I head for the elevator that will take us up to our suites.

As we stand side by side, I can feel she's uncomfortable near me. When the elevator opens, we step in, only the two of us, alone.

"Hey," I venture.

"Hey," she murmurs, avoiding my gaze.

"I'm sorry I snapped at you."

She says nothing, only looks at the ceiling.

"Right. Well, there's that," I snap again.

Damn it. I'm never gonna get anywhere with her if I can't stop being a dick.

We reach the top level and Daniella stomps out, after the elevator doors crawl open.

"Daniella, wait." I follow close behind her as the elevator door seems to slam shut.

She whirls to face me then jabs her fingernail into my chest. "You know what I don't like about you, Antonio Michaels?"

Too intimidated to talk, I just shake my head.

"I don't like how you can be *so* fucking dismissive." She jabs again. "I sensed something was bothering you and wanted to help. And instead of allowing me the opportunity, you just dismiss me, like I'm a little piece of shit."

Okay. I may deserve this.

But I can do without all of the jabs.

"My set director broke his leg and shattered his elbow while skiing. So now, with the show literally a few days away, I have no one to help coordinate backstage activities." I lean back against the hallway wall, beginning to feel nauseous.

"Oh my, Antonio. That's horrible." She approaches me and places her hands on my shoulders—no jabs to my chest this time, thank goodness. "Let me help."

"How?" I ask, mesmerized by the thick lashes that cradle her eyelids.

"Lucky for you, when I worked at Fashion Week in New York three years ago with Lauren Blake, that's what I did." Her hands move from my shoulders to my chest.

"And you're confident you can take on this project to the fullest?"

She cocks her head to the side and her eyes sparkle with a hint of playfulness. "Antonio Michaels, haven't I told you several times before, I never leave home without my confident panties?"

This is it. And fuck, I'm nervous. I don't even know why I opened up my big mouth three days ago, offering to step in for Ramon as the set director. I mean, it's been years since I was backstage at a fashion show.

So much to do.

But I'm game.

Liza has been a doll. We went shopping, and together, we found everything on my list to match the sketches for the accessories and complementary clothing for the show. Jonah has also been helpful, putting together the video presentations that will be displayed on the screens behind the runway.

But I have had to keep Liza and Jonah separate because either they argue over stupid shit, like which shade of blue something is, or they become engrossed in conversations as if they are in their own little world.

Antonio has been supportive, giving me an endless supply of funds to do all that I can to make this work. Yesterday, I reviewed all of the show details with him and he seemed pleased.

I know he's got a lot riding on today, so I can understand his apprehension.

We're up next—closing the show. All models are in place, ready to go strut their butts to Donna Summer's *She Works Hard for the Money.* They are all carrying briefcases and are wearing blazers, neckties, stilettos, *CraveMe* panties, and matching cleavage-enhancing demi-bras. Their hair is in sleek buns and they all have black-rimmed glasses. Nonna saw them when she came backstage to say hello, and she got a kick out of the ensembles—especially the glasses.

Nine songs later, models are prepared for their final walk tonight—to Madonna's *Express Yourself.* And what better way to 'express yourself' than to do so wearing sheer negligees and teddies in strappy heels while being escorted by hot topless guys with oil-slicked chests, tight jeans, and boots?

They all look perfectly naughty.

WHEN IT'S ALL OVER, THE FASHION SHOW ATTENDEES GIVE Antonio a standing ovation, and when he pulls me out there with him, the crowd gets louder. The experience is truly gratifying.

And now that it's over, all I want to do is curl up and take a long nap.

"Daniella. You're amazing. Thank you for making sure my designs stand out like superstars," Antonio says, lifting me up and embracing me.

"I had fun. Believe me, they would have stood out on their own. They're so exquisite."

"Come on. We still have to change for The Ball. I know you're tired, so we don't have to stay long. We can even leave after the first set of photos in the showcase photo shoot."

"Photo shoot?"

"Yes." He chuckles. "But you have nothing to worry about. I can tell the camera favors you. Just look at how many times TMZ has posted photos of you."

I lightly punch him in the gut and he hunches over in laughter.

We take the elevator up to our floor and, when we hop off, he lets me know he'll pick me up in two hours.

I lie down for about fifteen minutes before I finally peel myself off the bed and jump in the shower.

The warm water feels good as it hits my skin and aching muscles. Stress has made my body tense over the last few days and now that the fashion show is over, I feel some of that tension subside. However, I'm a little stressed about The Ball—mainly what I'll be wearing, coupled with the fact I'm going as Antonio's date.

I have to admit I'm getting into him. He's quite an irresistible hottie.

I step out, dry off, and blow-dry my hair, deciding to go for a sophisticated up-do, which I start to do when my phone rings.

It's Emma via FaceTime.

"Hey there! Is everything okay?" I ask straight away. It's only 5 a.m. there. Her calling early makes me worry a bit.

"Yes, D." She rolls her eyes. "It's just been hard to catch you at a good time, so I set my alarm to be sure I'd get you. I miss you."

"I miss you too, babe. But I'll be home tomorrow. We fly out early tomorrow morning."

"It's raining pretty bad. Aren't you landing in New York first?" Emma's eyebrows form into a worried furrow as she lays down under her covers.

"Yep," I mumble, as I begin to put on makeup.

"Well, I think a storm is headed there." Emma's sharp tone is wreaking with urgency.

I stop putting on my makeup to look into the screen. "Oh, well. I'm sure it will all work out. How's school? Have you been doing homework?"

"Of course. I do want to get into college, you know." She giggles. "Are you getting ready for The Ball?"

"Yes. I'll snap a selfie when I'm done." I wink.

"Okay. I bet Antonio is gonna kiss you tonight."

I shoot her a squinting glare. "Emma!"

She laughs hysterically like only a sixteen-year-old can.

"Well, have fun, D. Love you."

"Love you too."

After I finish my hair and makeup, I walk into the closet and remove the ensemble Antonio chose to showcase: a long, white halter-neck gown with a low plunge neckline, embellished by floral lace and soft mesh. It kind of captures an elegant balance of sheer seduction and femininity without being too revealing. The back is also low plunging with a flirty bow and the matching panty is also gold-trimmed. It's like the ultimate ball gown in the form of lingerie. It's quite inventive. And to accessorize the look, metallic leather high-heeled pumps with golden beads and crystal embellishments.

I feel honored that he asked me to wear it.

I just hope to God I look as good as he expects me to when he picks me up in less than ten minutes.

When he arrives at the door, I am a bundle of nerves. And when I lay eyes on him, I almost turn to mush.

Black tux. Perfect hair. Fucking hot.

His eyes brighten when he sees me. I can think to say is, "Don't I look swagalicious?"

He takes both my hands into his and says, "Actually, Daniella, I was thinking more like Princess-ish. At least, something a princess might wear on her wedding night, anyway. You look absolutely elegant, captivating, and enchanting."

CHAPTER 27

DANIELLA

The Ball is held at Fabrique, a large venue in Milan where concerts are held. Antonio steps out of the hotel limo first and then, like a gentleman, helps me out. The flash of cameras snapping photos startles me, but Antonio shields my face as he whisks me past photographers and through the grand entrance.

"Thank you for that. I don't think I will ever get used to being photographed so many times. How do you stand it?" I ask, as Antonio leads me through a sea of beautifully decorated tables.

"I don't stand it, actually. I'd give anything if they'd just leave me be."

We make it to a cloth-covered oval table that faces the stage and the dance floor. It is tastefully decorated with a feathered gold-and-white centerpiece surrounded by votive candles.

He pulls out a chair. "Here you go, lovely lady. Have a seat, please."

The entire venue décor gives off an enchantment vibe with golden lights streamed overhead and golden star-shaped confetti dusted on the tables and the floor.

Antonio takes his seat next to mine, and two other designers join us. "Hello, Sir Antonio. Your designs get better and better each year," one says while the other one nods.

Antonio smiles, leans into me, and whispers, "You look nervous."

"I'm not," I fib.

Truth is, I am nervous. I have never been to a ball before. Or maybe I'm just nervous being Antonio's date. It's a lot to take in, actually.

As the night moves along, we are served an exquisite meal of *Risotto alla Milanese* before I'm introduced to top designers. Photographers have taken at least twenty-seven photos of me while Antonio walks around, mingling with attendees as we are served bottomless glasses of champagne. I'm in awe by some of the designs showcased tonight. This is certainly an event I won't soon forget.

The venue lights dim and Antonio leads me back to our table. "Concert time," he says.

Music blares…a beat I'm all too familiar with.

Bruno Mars.

Lights illuminate the stage as Bruno sings his latest song. I shimmy my shoulders to the beat, and notice the ball attendees rise from their seats and make their way to the dance floor.

Antonio removes his tuxedo jacket and bow tie and places them both on the table. "Hey, you wanna dance?" He takes my hand and leads me to the dance floor.

"Um, I guess I don't really have a choice?" I chuckle.

Antonio's presence is entrancing, and I can feel his intoxicating gaze upon me, even though I refuse to look at him because his shirt is partially unbuttoned, tactfully teasing his muscular build.

I feel giddy and tipsy, especially since I've had at least four glasses of champagne. Two is usually my limit.

We continue to get our boogie on and I discover Antonio is quite a gifted dancer.

Bruno begins to sing one of his slow songs and Antonio pulls me closer, causing my entire body to shiver.

Please, get a hold of yourself, woman.

With my head now pressed lightly against his chest, I can't even concentrate on the song in the background. The sound of his heartbeat drowns out all other relative noise, creating its very own tune that the two of us erotically sway to.

Boom. Boom-boom. Boom. Boom-boom.

Is he as nervous as I am being this close to each other? If so, he sure conceals it just as well as a crooked politician conceals his deepest and darkest secrets.

If we could remain like this forever, I wouldn't protest. But only under these precise terms and conditions, without any words between us. No words whatsoever. Just silence. And our own private thoughts left unrevealed to no one but our very own inner consciences. Words lead to discoveries. And right now, I want what I am starting to feel inside for him and what I highly suspect he may be feeling for me, left undiscovered.

What am I so afraid of?

"Hey, you." Antonio's hum breaks up the battle between my head and my heart. He lifts one hand from around my waist and grabs a gentle hold of my chin, raising it off his chest. "You're super quiet tonight. Everything okay?" He kisses my forehead and smiles.

My flesh tingles and my knees weaken. The comfortable look in his eyes when they meet mine is electrifying. "Yes, I'm great!" I manage to say.

Somehow.

"You're shivering."

Yes. And it's all your fault.

"I know. I can't help it."

Please stop talking and just hold me, I silently plead.

"Daniella," he mutters, his deep voice soft and soothing. *Don't talk…*

With my hands interlocked in a soft embrace around his neck, I stare at him in anticipation of what I know is coming. He holds me even closer, his prominent hands wrapped around my waist. Bruno and his band continue to play soft tunes, and I feel a divine mix of dizziness and euphoria. Euphoria: Antonio and this moment. Dizziness: all of the champagne I've consumed throughout the evening. By now, I've had at least two more glasses, which for me is pretty outrageous.

"I-I," he stutters, pauses for a second, and clears his throat. "I think I'm fa—"

I interrupt his inevitable words by kissing him. Long and soft. I don't want to hear any more words. We stand in a long embrace, kissing without a care between us. I shiver again. Not because I'm cold, but because his hands slowly, yet strategically, move from the middle of my back, down my lower back, landing safely on my ass—*and I want more.*

Antonio's soft lips move from my open mouth to my ear. "You're cold and it's late. Let's leave. I'll get you to your hotel room," he whispers.

I quickly nod in agreement and, on my first step toward our table, I stumble. Again, *way* too much champagne.

"You're tipsy." He chuckles before kissing my forehead. He leads the way to our table to retrieve our belongings—my clutch and his tuxedo jacket and tie.

He drapes his jacket around my shoulders and lifts me up in his arms. "I'll carry you. You're in no condition to walk anywhere."

I open my clutch, remove my room key, and hand it to him. "I'm giving you full custody of getting me into my hotel room safe and sound."

Like a knight in shining armor, he carefully carries me outside and down a short flight of stairs to the hotel limo that is waiting for us. I feel so comfortable in his arms and comfortable in the moment. When we sit down in the limo, I instinctively rest my head on his shoulder and close my eyes.

And at this moment in time, I think I could be falling in love with him.

It has to be the champagne.

THE SOUND OF MY PHONE CHIMING AWAKENS ME EARLY THE NEXT morning. I open my eyes and reach for it. *Silence,* is all my pounding head keeps begging for. I turn off the alarm then close my eyes and immediately open them in a trance-like panic. I look around and instantly realize I'm still fully dressed: showcase ensemble, shoes…*everything*. I'm not even on the bed. I'm on the couch. My head is pounding, and I remember having an extremely naughty sex dream about Antonio last night.

Wait, was it a dream?

Champagne. Antonio. The kiss.

Oh, God. Did anything more than that kiss happen between us? Surely Antonio wouldn't take advantage of a woman who was smashed out of her mind, right?

I force myself up from the couch and a piece of paper falls onto the floor—a handwritten note from Antonio.

DANIELLA,

I wanted to see you safely to your room, and mission accomplished. Please text me when you wake up. We do have an 10 a.m. flight to catch.

Thank goodness he *is* a gentleman.

CHAPTER 28

ANTONIO

I wanted her so bad.

When she stepped out wearing my revealing show-case ensemble, I felt *everything* immediately rise to attention.

Sensual. Tempting. Daniella.

Her provocative appeal makes it harder and harder for me to resist. And believe me, after seeing her last night, I no longer care to resist.

But she had way too much to drink, and even though that kiss we shared was passionate, I'm a gentleman first. I brought her back to her room, carried her inside, laid her down on the couch, and left her a note. I even set her alarm clock on her phone so she would wake up in time for our flight to New York this morning.

But she seems annoyed with me now. As if I've done something wrong. She hasn't said much since I picked her up from her room. Only a few yes's and no's.

And a lot of arm-folding and scoffs.

We check our luggage in and get through customs, making it to our departure gate with only minutes to spare before we are called to board.

Our seats are in first class again, next to each other, and I do hope her mood settles soon, since we are in for a long flight.

Liza and Jonah aren't flying back until Saturday as they are staying for the full Fashion Week. I hope they learn to get along. They've been arguing non-stop, it seems.

"Is something wrong?" I finally get the nerve to ask.

"Nope. Not at all." She dishes up pursed lips and a cold shoulder.

"Great. Because I was beginning to think you're annoyed at me." I roll my eyes.

Could she be mad about that kiss? I don't want to bring it up unless she does.

The flight attendant makes the pre-take-off announcements, sounding much like the one we had on the flight here. I lean into the aisle and notice that it *is* her.

Daniella emphatically fastens her seat belt, then grabs a magazine, whipping through pages faster than she can read them. She then closes the magazine and shoves it back into the seat pocket.

"What's the matter?" I ask, with a questioning glare.

She folds her arms and then leans over to me. "I had a very heated sex dream about you last night, Antonio Michaels." She grimaces.

I can't help but laugh out loud. "So you're mad at me because you had a naughty dream about me?"

She nods. "Yep."

"And why are you mad at *me*?"

"I don't know." She pouts.

I lean in closer to her and say low and soft, "Was I any good, at least?"

A smile creeps up on her lips and before I know it, we laugh together.

"Look, thank you for being my date last night. There was no way in hell I would have let anything happen between us after we both had been drinking. I'm not that kind of guy. Even though you did look beyond gorgeous."

She gives a half-grin. "You didn't look too bad yourself."

"So, you're not mad anymore?"

"Nah. I was just feeling sexually deprived." She chuckles.

Welcome to my world.

We both fall fast asleep, for I don't know how long, before we are awakened by turbulence.

"Ladies and Gentlemen, we are experiencing heavy turbulence on our approach to New York City. Please make sure your seat belts are fastened and your tray tables are in their upright positions. Thank you."

Daniella stretches and lets out a yawn. "Looks like we were both tired. We didn't eat or anything."

"Yep. It's been a long week of events. I was wiped out."

The plane dips a little as it goes over an air pocket. Daniella grabs my arm.

"Ladies and Gentlemen, this is your captain. It looks like we are flying through a storm headed for New York and surrounding areas. All flights out of New York this evening have been cancelled. Please be sure to check with your individual airlines for more information."

Daniella's eyes dart. "Cancelled? What are we going to do? Where will we go?"

I pat her thigh and her expression softens. "Don't worry. I actually have an apartment here in the city. We can gather our luggage and head there and figure stuff out in the morning."

Daniella lets out a sign of relief and sits back in her seat, still gripping my arm.

After more turbulence during the final descent, we finally land. Daniella and I pick up our luggage at baggage claim, and haul it over to the rental car counter to rent a car. Then, we stop at the ticket counter and arrange for travel back out tomorrow afternoon, giving the storm time to pass.

"Come on, let's head to my apartment."

❦

DANIELLA LOOKS TIRED, HUNGRY, AND SLIGHTLY AFRAID. I WANT to do my best to ensure I make her feel protected. We stopped for Chinese takeout since we missed out on our meal on the plane.

"It's not even raining here. Why did they cancel flights?" she asks as we walk up the stairs to my apartment.

"Because the storm is headed here from the west. We will be fighting weather the whole way back to California. They had to cancel to be safe."

She offers a half-shrug. "Okay, I suppose."

Inside, my apartment it's cold. I haven't been here for months, so it may take a while to warm up.

Daniella looks around and smiles. "You have great taste, Antonio. Here and at your home in Beverly Hills." She starts to remove her coat and then decides against it after she shivers. "Is there only one bedroom?"

"The heat should kick in soon. And yes, only one bedroom. But you can have it. I'll sleep on the couch."

She chuckles. "I won't bite."

Yes, but I might.

CHAPTER 29

DANIELLA

A few hours passed as we ate dinner and showered before saying our goodnights.

Antonio's retired to the couch and I have retired to his bed.

Storms.

My worst nightmare.

Lightning flashes across the sky and seconds later the roar of the thunder makes my skin crawl.

Ashamed of being frightened, I lie here, still, aside from my heartbeat that reverberates throughout my entire being.

Go get Antonio. He'll keep you company. He knows thunderstorms scare you, remember?

Only, I'm too afraid to move. What if he laughs at me? Sends me back in here? I'd much rather hide under the covers all alone than be turned away.

Boom.

Another roar of thunder.

I can hear the howling cry of the wind whip past the window as if it's running, trying to seek its own shelter from the blooming storm.

Lightning again. This time, three flashes; one immediately after the other, as if they're playing a game of tag.

Crash!

I leap up out of the bed and race for the door that separates Antonio and me.

Fuck!

I'm naked.

I've gotta consider a nightgown or even a plain T-shirt from now on.

I reach for my robe and slip it on, trying to tie it closed as I swing the bedroom door open.

Antonio flies in, his hand on the knob, at the same time the door opens. *Oops.*

"Oh. I was just coming to check on you. Are you all right?" he asks.

"Oh, …" I stammer, not wanting to admit I'm scared. "I was coming to ask you—well, it's the window. I think it may be open a little. I can hear the wind howling."

Antonio walks over to the window and my heart thumps. He's shirtless and, through the flashes of lightning, I can see the solid form of his body.

Ripped *everything*.

My breathing intensifies, but I'm no longer sure it's because of the storm.

He walks away from the window and back over to me as I take shelter against the wall by the door. "The window is closed. Are you sure you're okay? Would you like me—?"

Boom.

The sound makes me bolt into Antonio's arms and he instinctively wraps them around me. "Daniella, you don't have to be afraid. I'm here with you."

I lean into the plane of his chest and can hear his heart beating just as fast as my own.

He lifts my chin and I meet his gaze, desire looming in his eyes. "Daniella, I—"

Boom.

I scream, and he leans into me as I back up against the wall again.

He runs a smooth fingertip along my face and fans his lips close to mine. "Shh. It's okay," he murmurs.

The sensation of him so close ignites me.

Oh, God. I don't want to want him.

But I do.

I can feel the loose tie of my robe come undone, exposing my nakedness.

The flashes of lightning darting through the window are like strobe lights, illuminating the skin on my bare body.

Antonio's eyes gleam and he leans even closer into me and whispers, "Why. Are. You. *Naked?"*

I breathe in quicker breaths. "I sleep naked, remember?" I manage to whisper back.

His breathing quickens too, as his eyes give my exposed body an obvious perusal. "Damn it, Daniella, you are so fucking beautiful. And I must add," he says as his lips graze over my exposed collar bone, "sleeping naked could be rather convenient."

"Not really. Not if there's a fire." My voice cracks as I try to conceal my nervousness.

His hand makes its way to my breasts and he cups one, running circles around my nipple with his thumb. "True. But it's certainly convenient for the man lucky enough to share a bed with you."

"Right. Only, I've sworn off men," I quip, feeling a flirtatious smirk formulate.

"Pity...How will you find pleasure?" His voice is deep and low, and, through the flashing bolts, I see his chest rise up and down as he continues to breathe faster.

"Perhaps I'll pleasure myself."

He grabs a hold of my hips, pulling me in, closer to him.

"Fuck, that's hot. Can I watch?" he says, his lips close enough for me to almost taste them.

I want to taste them.

"That's the second F-bomb you've dropped. Who's the Potty Mouth now, Mr. Michaels?"

He lifts me up, grabbing a hold of my exposed bottom, and I wrap my legs around his waist, sinking my nails into his back. He pushes closer into me, and I can feel the length of his hard cock trying to escape the confines of his silk pajama pants.

"What can I say, you must bring out the bad boy in me."

He stares into my eyes, then traces my lips with his tongue, teasing my mouth as my lips part on their own, begging for his tongue to play tango with mine.

The storm outside magnifies, mimicking what is building between us, and when he finally kisses me, I melt into him, internally begging for more. I'm hot all over, every inch of me soaring with need.

He abruptly pulls his lips away. "Daniella, I want you so bad. More than anyone I've ever wanted before. Please, baby, let me make love to you."

Oh. My. God. There goes swearing off men.

"I've wanted you since that kiss we shared at The Ball." I confess, almost breathless now.

He carries me over to the bed, the two of us falling into it, and I help him out of his pants, eagerly waiting to expose his cock.

I need him—this time for real.

No champagne-induced dream. No fantasy.

I welcome him in, between my thighs; they are shaky in anticipation of what's in store. He drops soft kisses along my belly, up to my breasts, causing me to arch into him. His lips meet mine and, together, our mouths impersonate the same dance of our lower bodies as we grind into each other, preparing for what we both want but are savoring until just the right simmering moment.

As he eases into me, thunder rumbles over us—the storm intensifying just as our lovemaking does.

The faster and more intense we are, the louder the thunder seems to roar.

Faster. Louder. Harder.

Shit, he's so damn good.

And when Antonio and I collectively explode in ecstasy, the rain outside finally falls.

࿐

THE STORM IS QUIET NOW AS ANTONIO AND I LIE FLESH-TO-flesh, still kissing, nothing but longing passion between us.

It's the first time I've ever been unfazed by an angry storm. The first time anyone has cared enough to comfort and hold me.

My eyes are wet, slightly welled with tears—not because I'm sad. Tears of elation because, for the first time, my heart feels *alive*.

Antonio's tender lips move from mine over to my earlobe that he playfully nibbles on as he caresses my breast with one hand and rubs my thigh with his other.

His touch keeps my heart racing.

Soothing. Caring. Affectionate.

He breathes softly in my ear and says, "Daniella, baby, I love you."

CHAPTER 30

ANTONIO

The words flew out my mouth without a second thought.

Natural. Unfiltered. Real.

I love her—since the first day I saw her, perhaps. On that Metro, her potty mouth and all.

Last night was indeed the best night of my life, as I explored every inch of Daniella's sensually perfect body—and God, how good it felt when she explored every solid inch of mine.

She shed a tear our first time and later explained how much it meant to her that I held her and made her feel safe during the storm. She's filled with hurt, and even though I'm dying to know why, last night was not the night for those type of discoveries.

Our flight back to Los Angeles is in less than an hour. I sprinkle soft kisses across her face as the two of us wait in line for coffee at a kiosk near our departure gate. We are both still tired, failing to sleep at all last night, making love as the storm passed through.

Thunder. Rain. Passion.

She smiles up at me, and although she has yet to tell me she loves me, her eyes tell me so.

Who would have thought TMZ had it right? Although we were never quite enemies, we were sure as hell destined to become lovers.

We order our coffees and head to our departure gate, the agent calling out for first class passengers to board, and, the instant we are seated, I get up the nerve to ask her what's on my mind.

"Am I gonna need to hire a new Personal Assistant?"

She looks up, her trademarked smart-ass smirk coming in for a hard landing. "Afraid you won't be able to keep your hands off of me at the office?"

I serve her a curveball smirk in return. "Baby doll, that's nothing new. That was a concern of mine from day one."

She raises an eyebrow and leans in closer; her flash of cleavage sends me back to last night when I tasted her nipples for the first time. "You can tell me I have to wear short, tight skirts with no panties every day, then spend your lunch hour feasting on my p—"

"Daniella Belle!" I interrupt, placing my index finger over her lips. I seriously contemplate taking her into the first class restroom for a personal induction into the mile-high hall of fame.

She giggles and grabs a hold of my finger moving it off of her soft lips. "I was only going to say *picnic lunch*. You can feast on my picnic lunch that I lovingly pack every day." She jabs her manicured finger into my bicep. "Seriously, Mr. Michaels, you should really get your head out of the gutter."

This woman…

She's *everything* I need.

Playful. Beautiful. Smart.

"Well, it seems you didn't mind my head in the gutter last night."

The old lady, sitting in the row across from us, squeezes her legs shut and shakes her head.

"Mr. Michaels!" Daniella says.

Of course I can't resist planting a kiss on her already puckered lips.

The flight attendant's announcement startles our locked lips free, and we both sit back into our own seats, waiting for the plane to take off, as we hold hands, our fingers tightly interlocked.

We fall asleep again, waking up right before the plane descends for a landing. And when we exit the plane and arrive at the busy spot to claim our baggage, I move in close to Daniella and whisper, "Will you please come home with me?"

She looks up at me, surprised. "I'd like that very much."

Truth is, I want Daniella to come home with me every single day. For the rest of my life.

TRAFFIC WAS A NIGHTMARE, AND ALL I COULD THINK ABOUT during the whole drive home was how much I wanted to run into the house and pour into Daniella. And the minute we walked through the front door, we didn't even make it all the way up the stairs before we ripped each other's clothes off, feverishly gaining access to our naked bodies—gifts to our stored-up desire.

Then I carried her into my room and onto my bed, where we still lie. I swear there is no end to the amount of times I can pleasure this woman. Seeing her react to every touch, lick, and thrust; her body is like a sexual sergeant—keeping me standing hard at attention.

AFTER OUR NAP, WE SHOWER AND HEAD TO THE KITCHEN TO prepare something to eat.

"Maybe we need to order takeout. I've got nothing in the fridge—all of the salami is gone."

"Chinese?" she says, perched up on the kitchen counter looking too adorable in my bathrobe.

"Chinese, it is."

We head to the living room after the takeout arrives and we eat it in front of the fireplace.

She looks at me inquisitively. "Nonna shared how she came to raise you in this house."

"Yep, she did. I've lived here all of my life." I dip an egg roll into sauce and feed it to her.

"It's a lovely home, that's for sure."

I shrug. "I suppose. But honestly, I'd take a small home away from the city, any day. Some guys have goals of living in lavish homes with a wife and kids. And in ironic contrast, I dream of a *modest* home with a wife and kids."

She nods as I feed her more egg roll.

"And you? What dreams of family life do you have, Daniella?"

Her eyelids sag and she doesn't say a word at first. "I've never had dreams of a family life," she utters as she looks at me with afflicted eyes.

I swallow hard. "Why is that?"

She glances at the ceiling, tugging at the end of her braided ponytail. "My parents were young when they had me and couldn't always afford to take care of me. I remember when I turned five, we were all living in a shelter when I was placed in foster care, with a promise they'd come back for me soon. Only they never did." Tears that shimmer in her eyes run slowly down her cheeks each time she blinks. "I grew up waiting for them to come for me. Every car that pulled up to my foster home, every phone call, I hoped it was them. When

I realized they weren't coming, I lost all hope in the idea of family, figuring they didn't love me enough."

I listen to her, open and vulnerable, realizing this is why she's so hurt. With her parents abandoning her, the idea of love became tainted to her so long ago. She no doubt never dreamed of family life, having had no sense of it growing up, and with the foster mom who didn't even care enough to comfort her in a thunderstorm, she'd probably grown up feeling unloved her entire life.

I reach for her, and pull her into my arms, holding her as she sobs. "Daniella, my baby, I'm so sorry."

I hold her for as long as she needs me to before we go back to my room. We don't even make love; we just lie naked in each other's arms and fall fast asleep.

CHAPTER 31

DANIELLA

Bedroom eyes.

That's what Antonio stares at me through when he looks at my naked body—his mega-seductive bedroom eyes.

And it's hot.

I must admit, we've been like two energizer bunnies since we first made love in New York.

He's kind of hard to resist, and when I playfully try to, he brandishes his dreamboat smile as if it's his panty-dropping arsenal.

And it is.

It's early and Antonio has left to get us some breakfast, so I shower, slip into one of his T-shirts, and head downstairs for the kitchen.

It's been a few days since I've spoken to Stacy and Emma so I decide to ring them via FaceTime.

"O.M.G., woman. Where are you? Are you still at his house sexing it up?" Stacy mumbles as she looks into the screen, toothpaste all over her mouth.

"Shhh. I don't want Emma to know what I've been doing." I blush, feeling embarrassed.

Stacy shoots off a lopsided grin. "Uh. You mean *who* you've been doing? Come on. She's almost seventeen. She knows."

"Are you both racing to head out the door?" I say, changing the subject.

"Yep. Welcome to our new life—post Daniella. It's horrible fending for ourselves now." She cackles, knowing I hate her sarcasm.

"Where is Emma?" I ask, swiveling in the barstool.

Stacy sighs. "I'm headed to her room now, love. Hold on."

Seconds later, Emma, with her happy grin, pops into the screen.

"Hi, D." The corner of her mouth quirks up. "Please come home. Mom is driving me mad. Honestly, she doesn't know our routine."

Stacy pops back into the picture armed with an expressive eye-roll. "See what you left me here with? Nothing but pure attitude. She's like a younger you."

I laugh. "Oh, no. She's all you, believe me."

Emma appears again. "D, how's your love life? Didn't I tell you that you'd come back from Milan all in love? I should have bet money on that. Or those pink high heels of yours I love so much." Her long lashes flutter.

I fold my arms and raise my chin defiantly. "Don't mind me, young lady. How is school?"

"It's fine, D. And I met a guy. He's invited me to prom already." Her eyes brighten.

"Did he? That sounds kinda cool."

Emma's eyes widen and she giggles. I realize Antonio has returned and he's standing behind me.

"Hey, there. You must be Emma? I'm Antonio."

Emma nearly passes out and Stacy shows her face. "Hey, Antonio, I'm Stacy. You better be good to Daniella."

"Stacy!" I interject.

Antonio chuckles. "It's good to meet you, Stacy. And yes. I

will be very good to Daniella." He squeezes the side of my waist.

I feel my face warm. "Well, you two have a great day. I'll be home soon. Love you."

"Love you, too," they both shout before I end the Face-Time call.

Antonio plants a kiss on my cheek. "I bought us some coffee and donuts."

"Donuts?"

"Yep. I thought it would be cute if we ate some jelly donuts. You know, to commemorate that day on the Metro. The day I first laid eyes on you." He winks and brandishes that damn smile.

Only this time, that smile won't get me to drop my panties.

Because I'm not wearing any.

I hop onto the center island counter. "You mean the day you laid your jelly donut on me?" I giggle.

He eases his way in-between my thighs and moves his hands underneath the T-shirt, up my back. "You're wearing my T-shirt." His soft hiss ignites my…*everything*.

I deliver a playful side-eye then grab the bottom half of the T-shirt and lift it up and over my head, peeling it off. "No, I'm not."

He looks at my naked body hungrily, as if he's licking me with his eyes.

I give a half-smile and say, "Aren't you gonna eat breakfast?"

"Fuck, Daniella," he growls. "This is the kind of shit that makes me want you so bad." His breaths quicken as he cups my face and pins soft kisses on my open mouth, teasing me with his tongue.

"Then have me. Right here. Right now."

A sultry laugh escapes him. "Oh baby, I have every intention of having *all* of you. Right here. Right now."

He licks his way down to my center and before I know it, he's feasting on my pussy as I lie sprawled out on the counter, losing my mind in his sensational lick, flick, and stroke method.

Lick. Flick. Stroke.

And as I reach my eye-rolling climax, I realize I could very well be the luckiest woman in Beverly Hills.

TIME CERTAINLY FLIES WHEN YOU'RE HAVING FUN—AND TOE-curling sex.

I feel euphoric, imagining how Anastasia Steele must have felt when she was all sexed-up by Christian Grey.

Without all of the kinky rough sex and BDSM, of course.

A very reluctant Antonio took me back to Stacy's house this evening. It's Sunday now, and I figured since we have work tomorrow, a night apart may do us some good after having been sprawled together for the last three days. I admit, I miss him already. His lovemaking is out of this world.

Sensual. Commanding. Addicting.

He's mentioned he loves me several times now.

I want to believe he does, but I know true love doesn't exist.

CHAPTER 32

ANTONIO

I couldn't sleep.

Having spent time with Daniella in Milan, and then intimately for the past few days and nights, not having her with me last night was unbearable.

I'm at my downtown office now, earlier than usual, keeping myself busy before everyone arrives. Daniella insisted on arriving on her own today so as not to call attention to us. Frankly, it's my company and I couldn't care less what others think or draw conclusions about. But I want her to feel as comfortable as possible.

Familiar voices and giggles take me to the front of the office where I'm surprised to find Liza and Jonah.

"Hey, guys," I say, happy to see them both...although I'm not sure what brings Jonah to my office this early.

"Oh," Liza says, a smile plastered on her face. "You're here early, boss." She sits at her desk and begins to shuffle through paperwork.

I nod and look to Jonah. "Did you two come here together?"

"Oh, well, I-I came to see you here and uh, we...me and Liza walked in the building at the same time."

"Oh, cool. Well, lucky for you I'm here early. Why didn't you just call me? I haven't heard from you since I left Milan."

"Well, we just got back Saturday. And I have a meeting with another client in the area. I wanted to drop this off here for you to look at. Figured I should do it while I'm in the area, whether you were here or not." He hands me a flash drive. "It's the video footage I captured of the fashion show. I want you to approve it when you can. I'd like to start on your new marketing campaign."

I turn to Liza. "How was the rest of Fashion Week? Did you enjoy Milan? I hope this guy didn't give you any problems."

She blushes. "Milan was fabulous, boss. Thanks for allowing me to go."

"So"—Jonah claps his hands together—"I'm just gonna head out now. I'm glad I caught you here this early."

"Sure. Me too. I'll walk you down to your car. I've got something to tell you."

"Oh, okay." He looks at Liza. "It was nice running into you. Have a great day."

"Yep. You have a great day too, Jonah," she says, now looking at her computer screen.

I follow Jonah out to the elevator and, when inside, decide to fill him in on what's transpired between me and Daniella. I mean he is my best bud.

"So, uh things happened between me and Daniella."

Jonah looks up from the elevator floor. "What? Well, I can't say I'm really surprised. I mean you've been hot for her since you saw her. And I'm sure she was a beauty at The Ball. Did it happen then?"

We exit the elevator, and I fill Jonah in on some details, albeit leaving out the intimate ones. Once we reach his car I say, "I told her I love her."

Jonah's eyes widen. "Fuck yeah, man! It's about time your ass is in love. So, does this mean you finally found *her*?"

I glance at the sky, the sun peeking through the clouds ever so covertly. "I'm pretty sure she's the one." I smile and Jonah grabs my hand, pulling me into a man hug.

"Congrats, Antonio. I was worried about you for a minute there. You've only got a few months before you turn thirty. Does she know?"

I shake my head. "No way. Not yet."

"Well, I think you should tell her. And again, congrats; I think she's perfect for you. She keeps you in line." He cackles then glances down at his watch. "Gotta head out, man. Meeting in thirty minutes."

"Right. I'll look at the video and get back to you later. Thanks, Jonah."

As I walk back to the building, then ride up the elevator, I begin to think about my 30th birthday and Miss Tilly. Sure, I inherited her house and money, but since Miss Tilly never married and didn't want me to end up lonely like she was, she tied a stipulation to my inheritance. I need to be married before I turn thirty in a few months or I lose everything but the house. The money will automatically go to different organizations. It's a fact that's been hanging over my head for quite some time now, especially since at twenty-nine, I haven't found anyone I'd like to call my wife.

Until Daniella.

But oddly, I don't even care about the money. I've made my own since I started *CraveMe,* and haven't touched any of the money in my trust account except for donations I make to the hospital I was born.

Exiting the elevator, my phone buzzes.

I smile. A text from my girl.

Daniella: **I'm on my way. Stacy is headed downtown today and will drop me off. Shall I bring coffee?**

I'm glad she's getting a ride. She was to take an Uber even though I offered to allow her to use the Beamer I have parked in my garage.

Me: **No. And you need a car.**

Daniella: **No. I told you I hate driving in Los Angeles traffic.**

Me: **You're stubborn.**

Daniella: **That's not exactly breaking news, Mr. Michaels. But since we have resorted to pointing out the obvious... you're quite bossy.**

Me: **That's right. Now hurry up and get your sweet ass to work. I've missed you.**

CHAPTER 33

"**W**hy are you even here, D? You should be with *him*!" Emma exclaims the minute she walks into the kitchen and finds me making a sandwich.

I haven't been back to Antonio's since I came back home Sunday, and I guess Emma is finding an issue with that. She has been hinting all along I need to go be with him. I suppose now she's a little more emphatic about it. Honestly, I do miss spending intimate time with him. At the office, we've been able to keep it super-professional. And he's been working late, so I've just been coming home.

"Calm down there, girlie," I joke. "I am going to be with him. He had some errands to run and I wanted to pack some stuff."

She plops down onto the barstool with her arms folded. "Well, good then. You'd be a fool not to be spending time with him."

I lean into the counter and take a bite of my sandwich. "I know, right? He is quite dreamy."

Emma flutters her long lashes and lets out a whimsical sigh. "It's so romantic. I think he's in love with you."

"Don't try to analyze my love life, little girl. Would you like a sandwich?"

"No, thank you. I had pizza with Julian after school."

"Julian?"

"Yes. The guy I met. The one who's taking me to prom." She hops off the barstool and walks over to the fridge to grab a bottle of water.

"Oh, his name is Julian? Sounds sophisticated," I say through bites of my sandwich.

"He's really sweet, D. I want you to meet him."

"I will, babe. But for now, I've gotta go pack. Antonio will be here soon."

❧

ANTONIO PICKS ME UP AND TAKES ME BACK TO HIS HOUSE WITH plans for us to cook dinner together.

"Are you sure we'll be able to cook in here without ending up naked on the counter?" I ask playfully.

"As long as you don't strip down to your glorious naked-ness, like you did before." Antonio pulls me close and kisses my forehead. "Because the second I see you naked, all bets are off."

"Mmm-hmm," I say looking up at him. "Well, don't be flaunting any of your sexy-ass smirks that make me want to strip down to my nakedness."

"I'll try not to. But it's good to know that's all I have to do to get you naked."

We prepared what has become our favorite meal together —pizza, loaded with mushrooms, bell peppers, olives, and pepperoni, and gulped it down with a glass of red wine as we lounged in the living room and watched the movie he's never watched before—The Godfather.

"So, what did you think?" I ask after the movie is over.

He raises a skeptical eyebrow. "Well, besides the fact it

was long, I admit it's good. I'm glad you made me watch it." He smirks.

I lean in close to him and brush my lips against his. "Antonio, is that a smirk I see on your face?"

He pulls me on top of him on the couch. "You're very observant. Why aren't you naked yet?"

I lift myself off of him. "That, was not your *sexy* smirk." I laugh and run up the stairs, then into his room.

And when he catches up to me, he says, "How about we step into the jacuzzi."

"It's cold."

"Not inside the jacuzzi."

I don't even hesitate. "Fine. After you."

I strip down and slip into Antonio's bathrobe as he jets up the jacuzzi, then watch him undress and step in, testing the temperature before gesturing for me to join him.

I slip out of the robe and step in. "The water feels nice," I say, inching my way over to him.

When I sit down, he scoots over to me, nestling between my thighs.

Leaving a trail of soft kisses up my neck as he rubs my breasts, his mouth makes its way to mine. "Move in with me," he murmurs, his lips teasing my own.

"Move in with you?" I say, my legs trembling as his hand moves from my breast down my belly, his hand softly grazing my sex.

"Yes, baby. Move in with me. As in, live here."

I tremble, as he slides two of his fingers inside me, teasing my spot. "That's a serious step," I say through quickened breaths.

"And, I'm quite serious about you." He gently tugs at my bottom lip with his teeth.

I close my eyes, basking in the pleasure of his hand and fingers performing their magic under the warm jet-induced bubbles as I feel myself begin to lose control. "Yes, baby, yes," I shout as I give in to the pleasure.

He holds onto me as the orgasm moves through my mind body and even my soul.

"Was that a yes?" The hum of his voice sending more sensational heat through me.

When I *recover*, I open my eyes and look up at him. "Yes. Antonio. I'll move in with you."

THE NEXT MORNING, WHILE IN THE SHOWER, ANTONIO IS QUIET and seems deep in thought. He sticks his arm out to reach for something and tucks his arm behind his back.

Before I even have time to ask him what he's up to, Antonio Michaels gets down on one knee and presents a black box. He then slowly opens the box and I nearly pass out.

Inside the box is a huge ring, maybe ten carats. "Daniella Belle. Don't think I'm the type of man who would ask a woman to move in just for the hell of it. I freaking adore the hell out of you. I love you and want to spend the rest of my life with you. Will you marry me?"

I melt. "Fuck yes!"

CHAPTER 34

DANIELLA

It's been a couple of weeks since I've moved in with Antonio. I've been beside myself. Who would have ever thought I'd be engaged—to anyone—let alone Antonio Michaels?

It was hard, but I finally admitted I love him, doing so the day he proposed, and every day since. Love has been something difficult for me to embrace. It's hard for me to trust that someone loves me since my own parents abandoned me as a child. Likewise, it's hard for me to accept love, too afraid to trust anyone could ever love me.

But thanks to Antonio, that's all changed now.

Like all brides-to-be, I've been browsing bridal magazines, searching for the perfect dress. The date hasn't been officially set yet; Antonio has left that up to me. Stacy and Emma are going nuts, both excitedly helping me decide on where to hold the ceremony.

"How about a destination wedding? Bermuda...on the beach." Emma beams.

"No. What about something intimate, like at home?" suggests Stacy.

The two both shout, "I've got it!" at the same time,

sounding like they are the same person again, as they both grin through the screen via FaceTime.

I laugh. "Calm down, you two. Hold that thought until another time. I've gotta get off this call. I've been lounging around too much today. Antonio and I have a dinner date later."

"Oh, okay. Have lots of fun, D!"

"Yeah, what she said. Just call us later," says Stacy.

I clean off my desk; papers are scattered about since I've been working from home today. Antonio had meetings that, for the first time in a while, I didn't need to attend.

I shower and pick out a cute black dress to wear with the pink high-heeled strappy stilettos that I wore the day Antonio and I bumped into each other on the Metro.

The TV blares in the background and as I'm just about to blow-dry my hair, I hear Antonio's name mentioned on the program.

Curious, I walk out of the bathroom, then stare at the 55-inch screen of the TV that hangs over the fireplace in the bedroom.

TMZ has just come on and they are leading with a story about Antonio.

CraveMe *CEO, Antonio Michaels, was spotted a couple of weeks ago shopping for an engagement ring. Could it be because his 30th birthday is quickly approaching and he needs to get married by then, in order to keep his hefty inheritance?*

Shock riddles through my body and I suddenly feel cold.

I ease onto the edge of the bed and try to swallow the thick lump now lodged in my throat.

What. The. Fuck.

What do they mean he *needs* to get married by the time he turns thirty or he loses his inheritance?

He's never mentioned any of this to me before.

Can it be true? If it is, does this mean he's using me to keep his fucking money?

My phone buzzes. It's Stacy.

Ugh. I don't really want to talk right now.

I roll my eyes. "Hey," I say, my eyes still glued to the TV.

"Are you watching TMZ?"

"Yeah," I say, barely able to speak intelligently.

"I figured. Sweetie, don't believe what you see on their report. You know, firsthand, how sometimes these shows spin the truth."

Tears pool in my eyes and my mouth goes dry. "Yeah, but Stacy...suppose it's true?"

"Even if it's true, that doesn't mean what I'm sure I guess you're thinking. He's not using you to keep the money. I know he loves you. Anyone who has seen the way he looks at you, knows that."

Love can never be trusted.

"Right. Well, I'm gonna go now, Stacy. I'll call you later."

I feel sick to my stomach.

"Promise you'll call later?"

"Yep. I promise."

I wipe the tear that's managed to trickle its way down my cheek and I feel my heart rate speed up as I spiral into a panic.

You can't get your emotions in a bunch without knowing for sure if it's true.

I decide to call Antonio. Confront him. Hopefully he's done with his meeting. And as his phone rings, I feel a weird combination of butterflies and nausea brewing in my stomach.

He answers, "Daniella, baby, have you seen TM—"

I readily interrupt as I pace the bedroom floor. "Is it true?" I ask, my voice subdued.

"Baby, I can explain," he begins and that's all I need to hear.

It's *true.*

I hang up and the floodgate of tears emerge.

I knew it.

No such thing as love.

Who would love me anyway?

Unworthy. Unwanted. Daniella.

Should have stuck to swearing off men. I sure wouldn't be *here*. Faced with this bullshit.

I grab a suitcase, pack up whatever I can fit into it, throw on jeans and a shirt and leave, without looking back.

Destination: who the fuck knows—just far away from the crap-fest of *I love you* lies.

⚜

It's been a few hours, I guess. Maybe more. I've been in the same spot, for I don't know how long, since I checked into this hotel, walked into the room, and crashed onto the bed.

My phone is off. I don't want to speak to anyone. Yet, now that I think about it, I should text Emma and Stacy, at least.

As soon as I power my phone back on, I see there are twenty calls from Antonio, along with at least the same amount of text messages, which I ignore, and voicemails, which I don't listen to.

Leave me alone, liar.

I text Stacy to let her know I'm safe.

Stacy: **Okay. Glad you're safe, babe, but I'm worried about you. Antonio has been here looking for you. He doesn't look good.**

Me: **He's probably more upset about the fact he may indeed lose his inheritance.**

Stacy: **I'm not too sure about that. He really looked torn.**

Whatever.

Me: **I just wanted to tell you I'm safe. Please let Emma know, too.**

Stacy: **What are you going to do, love?**

Me: **I'll figure it out in the morning. But for now, I just** want to sleep. I'm turning my phone off. I don't want him to keep calling me. I'll call you tomorrow. Love you.

Stacy: **Love you more.**

SLEEPING WITH A BROKEN HEART IS ENTIRELY POINTLESS; I hardly recommend trying it.

I force myself out of bed, and when I make my way to the bathroom, I wipe my eyes free of tears, only to make room for more.

How could he do this to me?

I practically poured my fucking soul out to him—shared how hurt I was. He ate it up and tricked me into falling in love with him so he could reel me into some fake, *I got to keep my inheritance,* marriage.

It's true. The beautiful ones hurt you every single time.

But no more.

This is the last time I ever waste loving anyone.

CHAPTER 35

ANTONIO

S he's gone.
I literally can't breathe.
Never have I felt so alone.
Abandoned. Lost. Incomplete.

Like someone wandering in the desert without a single drip of water.

I've sent Daniella an endless amount of text messages, called her cell phone countless times, and have reached out to Emma and Stacy, both claiming to have no clue where she is.

I've cried. And for the record, there is no way I've *ever* shed a tear over a woman. My love for her is real. And she doesn't believe it.

It's been at least three days, I think. Truth is, I've lost track. I'm worried.

The only solace I have is the hope she'll have to return here someday, as most of her clothes are still hanging in her closet. I even tripped on those sexy pink heels she was wearing that day on the Metro.

How could she doubt my love for her?

I couldn't care less about that money. It's not like I need it.

I purposely didn't push Daniella for a wedding date because I don't care.

Nonna warned me to tell Daniella. So did Jonah. But, I didn't think it would surface.

Fucking TMZ.

Why can't they just leave me alone?

Nonna has called me at least three times today. I can't imagine the news report traveled all the way to Italy.

I call her back via speaker phone on my home office desk. I haven't left the house for a couple of days now...in fear I'll miss Daniella when she returns.

"*Nipote, come stai? Ho sentito la notizia.* Is everything okay?"

Seems the news *has* spread to Italy.

Ugh.

I bury my head in my hands. "No, Nonna. Everything is not okay. Daniella is gone. The news report upset her, and I suppose she thinks I asked her to marry me so I wouldn't lose the inheritance Miss Tilly left me."

"Oh no, Antonio. I'm so sorry. She'll come to her senses; just give her time. She's yours forever. Destiny won't let her get away."

"I sure hope you're right, Nonna." My voice cracks.

"Call me if you need anything. *Mi dispiace tanto per il dolore che stai provando, tesoro mio.*"

"*Grazie, Nonna. Ti voglio bene.*"

"Ciao. Ti voglio bene anch'io."

My grandma. Always the optimist.

Destiny won't let her get away.

God knows I want this to be true.

A knock at the door makes me jump in my seat and I leap up, eager to know if it's her.

"Daniella," I say, as I whip the front door open.

But it's Jonah. Carrying bags of fast food.

Fries. Burgers.

I couldn't eat even if I wanted to. Daniella is my sustenance. Food can wait.

"Hey, man." He grimaces. "Don't look so sad to see me."

I wave him inside. "I was hoping you were Daniella. But you're not."

"Nope. Just me. Coming to check on you." He raises the bags. "And I bought you some food. Remember that joint we used to go to? They have the best fries in town."

It does smell good.

"Yep. Well, thanks. I don't think I've had anything to eat since she left me."

We sit down on the barstools in the kitchen, and Jonah removes burgers and fries from the bags.

"No luck finding out where she is, huh?" He takes a hearty bite of his burger.

I shake my head and nibble on a few fries.

"Liza said she thinks she may still be at the Beverly Hilton."

I tilt my head to the side. "*Still*? Why would she say that? And when did you talk to Liza?"

Jonah looks down at his fries and dunks them into a pool of ketchup. "I, uh, dropped off the mock-up of your new campaign, and Liza and I started chatting about TMZ and Daniella—anyway she sent you a text. Didn't you read it?"

"I've been ignoring texts and calls from everyone who isn't Daniella."

"Well, she sent you a text yesterday. Apparently, Daniella called the office asking Liza if she could draft her a letter of recommendation. She was seeking other job opportunities and a letter from *CraveMe* would help."

"She did what?"

"Yeah. Only she didn't call from her cell phone. So Liza curiously dialed the number that showed up on the office Caller ID and it went to the front desk of The Beverly Hilton. Her guess is Daniella called from her hotel room, and when

Liza dialed the number back, it automatically looped to the hotel front desk."

I sink in my seat. I cannot believe this…The Beverly Hilton is only a few miles away.

"Man, you should really check your text messages. Liza said she texted you all the info. Plus, she said the hotel's housekeeping manager lives in the same building she does."

"You're shitting me. Seriously?"

He shakes his head. "Check your messages, man. It's all in there."

I pick up my phone and begin scrolling through messages.

Taking one last bite of fries, Jonah slides off the barstool. "Anyway, man. I just came to check on you and bring you some food. Call or text Liza, then go get your girl. But clean yourself up first." He pauses as he sips on some soda. "You really look like shit."

Jonah leaves and I sit, scrolling through a barrage of text messages. So many of them. Vendors. One from Uncle Carlo, even. And then I see Liza's. *I think I know where Daniella is.*

So this misery could have ended yesterday?

I text a reply.

Me: **Liza, sorry I missed this text. Do you think you know where Daniella is?**

A few agonizing minutes later, she replies.

Liza: **Yep. Jonah just gave me the heads-up you'd be contacting me. I'm on it, boss. I'll call my friend right now…see if I can get you a room number.**

Why is it that Jonah and Liza are like best buds now? They never said so much as one word to each other—Liza avoided him like the plague and they seemed to bicker the whole time in Milan. I'll tackle that super mystery as soon as I find my Daniella.

Me: **Great. I'll wait to hear back from you. And thanks, Liza.**

Jonah's right. I need to clean myself up. I've never looked this low.

Coffee stained T-shirt. Sweatpants with holes. Greasy hair.

If Daniella came back now, she'd leave me solely based on my raggedy-ass appearance.

❦

LIZA HASN'T TEXTED YET. I'VE BEEN SHOWERED AND DRESSED FOR what seems like forever, although it's probably been only an hour.

And finally, a text message comes through.

Liza: **Found her, boss. Beverly Hills Hilton Suite 1265. Good luck.**

Me: **You're a rock star, Liza. I'm giving you a raise and a promotion.**

Liza: **Cool!!**

Anxiously, I grab my keys and wallet then walk halfway out the door.

Shit. I forgot something.

I two-step it all the way to the top of the stairs, through the bedroom door, and into Daniella's closet.

I grab those sexy, pink, strappy heels—I've got an ingenious idea.

And now I'm in my car, racing to The Beverly Hilton to go get my girl.

CHAPTER 36

DANIELLA

I miss him.

As ironic as that may seem, I fucking miss him.

Is it possible to love and hate someone at the same time?

I'm thinking, yes. My heart loves while my mind is swimming with anger and hurt.

Part of me wishes he'd come rescue me—like a scene in one of those sappy romance flicks.

Honestly, if he'd just tell me we can wait as long as I'd like before we marry, then I'd know it's not about the money. Then I'd know he does indeed love me.

But that's a chapter people read at the end of fairy tales.

Fake shit like that doesn't happen in *real* life.

Not my life.

So after having a few days to come up with an epic plan, I've decided to leave. Pack up my stuff and start anew. I've got money saved up from working for Stacy, plus the money I earned working for Antonio. There's a fabulous position in Paris, working for the renowned Lauren Blake, and I took a chance and emailed her assistant, and Lauren, herself, got back to me right away. She remembers my work at New York

Fashion Week when I was in design school, and she'd be delighted if I joined her design team. My flight leaves tomorrow night.

Stacy and Emma are sad but still excited for me. Both have begged me to give Antonio a chance; however, my mind is made up. Paris is calling where I can start fresh.

No TMZ. No Antonio. No heart-breaking lies.

Stacy has agreed she'll be the one who'll reach out to Antonio and ask him to pack up my belongings, then she'll send them to me when I'm settled in France. I've arranged to stay in a charming flat with a woman called Annika who works for Lauren Blake. It's temporary, but at least it's a start.

I'm even getting a puppy. I hear a dog's love is unconditional. I'm in need of a good dose of that.

I'll say my good-byes to Stacy and Emma tomorrow, but tonight, I'll just chill.

Room service. Bubble bath. Sleep.

I even ordered a bottle of wine to go with my meal.

And finally, a knock on the door. Hopefully room service has arrived.

I unlock the door and fling it open.

Yes! It *is* room service with a cart full of kiss-my-sorry-ass-sadness-away goodness.

Pizza. Chocolate cake. Wine.

I pour myself a glass of wine even before the server sets my tray down on the table.

"Anything else, Miss?"

"Nope. That's it. Thank you."

I give him a tip. He smiles and offers his appreciation, then pushes the serving cart toward the door. Once I open the door for him, my mouth drops.

Antonio.

What. The. Hell.

How is he even here right now?

"Can I please come in?" His voice is light, while his blue eyes, that glisten, are fixed on mine.

I manage to nod and step aside as he walks in.

He reaches for my hand.

I pull away.

"Please don't touch me, Antonio."

He steps back, holding one hand up and one behind his back. "Okay. I won't touch you. But please let me explain."

"Nothing you say can change what I heard on that news report. You need to get married, and guess who was the naive one you reeled in to make sure that happens? Me. But it doesn't matter. I'm leaving for France tomorrow."

His shoulders sink. "What? France? Daniella. Baby, you—"

"Yep," I interrupt, taking a sip of wine. "Paris. To work with Lauren Blake."

He shakes his head. "I'll come with you."

What? *Totally unexpected.*

"I beg your pardon?" I ask, now sitting on the edge of the bed, losing my ability to stand without my knees shaking.

"It sounds like a wonderful opportunity for you. So I'll come with you. I can still operate *CraveMe* remotely. Heck, we can even open up our first boutique there."

We can open up *our* first boutique? Does he not remember I'm angry with him?

He moves his hand from behind his back. Holding up my pink shoes by their strap, he approaches me slowly, cautiously. "Once upon a time, I heard a story in which a man confirms his true love by slipping the shoe she left behind, on her dainty foot. If it fit perfectly then she was indeed his match...or something like that."

I feel my eyes well up with tears. "Is that supposed to be the story of Cinderella rescued by Prince Charming?"

He gives a cautious smile, inching in closer my way. "Kind of."

"Well, I thought you were my Prince Charming, but you proved he does not exist."

"Did I? I'm here now, aren't I?" His brows lift.

I swallow the painful lump in my throat as he gets closer, now on one knee, kneeling as he lifts my foot.

"And the fact that you need to get married?"

He scoffs. "Daniella, baby. You're right. I do need to marry…*you*. But, God knows, I don't need to marry you for any reason other than the fact I want to spend the rest of my life with you. I don't need the money. I've got that on my own and we can even marry *after* my 30th birthday. And I'd give up everything…for you, which is why I'm even willing to go to Paris. Together." He slips one shoe on my foot, and I sink my face in my hands, the tears coming harder than I expected them to.

Antonio lifts my chin and leans in close, his lips gently touching mine. "Just as I thought, baby, the shoe is a perfect fit. I'm Prince Charming-ish. And you're Cinderella-ish." His lips swoop over mine and we kiss.

Tender. Long. Passionate.

I'm melting inside and I can't help but think…this moment—this exact, fucking moment—is precisely what fairy tales are made of.

Our lips part momentarily and, like music to my ears, Antonio mutters, "This, Daniella my love, is where *we* begin our very own happily ever after.

"The Right Shoes Can Change Your Life."

— CINDERELLA

EPILOGUE

FATE

The groom, handsomely decked out in his tuxedo, surveys himself in the mirror with a satisfied grin.

This is the day you've been dreaming about, he says to himself.

Indeed true.

Since the first day he laid eyes on her, he knew *she* was the one.

Sure, it took a while for them to get to this point—with all of the obstacles thrown their way, he had to work harder than he ever expected to, convincing her *he* was the one.

It was certainly worth it, he thinks, as he begins to reflect back on events that led them here.

A knock on the door takes him away from the flashback of the day he proposed, reeling him back to now when, in less than twenty minutes, he will stand face-to-face with the woman he plans to spend all of his life with.

"You ready to make this whole thing legit?" his best man asks, looking equally handsome in his tux.

"I've *been* ready."

"Then, hurry up. Let's go."

The two walk out of the room and enter the church,

walking past the countless number of guests sitting on the bride's side and the groom's side—the bride wanted a huge wedding, and he felt it necessary to give her what she wanted.

The groom, now feeling just a tiny bit of nerves creep up, acknowledges the guests with a nod and a smile as he prances to the front.

He claims his spot among the best man and groomsmen, all facing the direction in which they expect to see the beautiful bride make an appearance and float down the aisle.

The best man leans in and says, "Dude, I still can't believe you're getting married before *me*." He chuckles.

The groom laughs. "I know, man, neither did I. But we didn't want to wait. And *you'll* be tying the knot soon."

"Yep. In just a few short weeks. I can't wait," the best man admits, grinning at the thought of his own wedding fast approaching.

The organist begins to play music, making this moment seem all too surreal.

The flower girl skips out, spreading love with rose petals as she trots down the aisle, her curls bouncing.

Giddy bridesmaids take turns stepping down the aisle now, and the groom feels his heart begin to sprint, knowing he soon will see her.

It's been a week since they last saw one another, the bride insisting they have some real time apart to prepare for this day.

It was a fair exchange, he thought, since he'd be able to spend every day with her, after saying I-Do.

The maid of honor now appears and slowly saunters down the aisle. She looks over to the groom, then the best man, and smiles as she claims her place next to the priest.

The organist pauses for just a minute before she begins to play the Wedding March—a symphony to the groom's heart.

Guests turn in their seats as they all wait for the bride.

They all gasp in awe, when she appears. The groom finds it hard to hold back tears filling his eyes at the sight of her—the woman of his dreams—walking toward him, looking even more beautiful as he imagined she would.

Bride and groom, both trembling, stand, holding hands as they face each other, both giddier than they expected to be. This was nothing like rehearsal. This was the real deal.

The priest, ready to perform the ceremony, asks if anyone thinks the two should not be joined together in holy matrimony, and a notable silence floods the room.

The bride and groom exchange the vows they personally wrote for this momentous occasion and soon enough, the priest says to the groom, "You may now kiss the bride."

Jonah leans in to kiss Liza, his beautiful new bride, and when they break free, he turns to face his best man, Antonio, and says, "By the way, you owe me a thousand dollars for wager-fest. You bet me I would get *nowhere* with Liza. And yeah…we're pretty much married now, dude ."

Everyone laughs in unison, including the little flower girl.

Jonah's lifelong motto has been: if you don't go after what you want, then you'll never have it.

Now, he's certainly got what he wanted. Liza and their fortuitous happily-ever-after.

And Daniella Belle and Antonio Micheals will have theirs too, in Paris, France. When they exchange vows on Antonio's 3oth birthday.

The End.

THANK YOU

Dear Lovely Reader,

Thank you for reading Cinderella-ish!! I hope you enjoyed Daniella and Antonio's Story as much as I enjoyed writing it!!

This story was inspired by not-so-true life events — but one thing is certain, my husband is my very own Prince Charming so I decided to dedicate this book to him and release it on our anniversary. Sweet and Mushy, right? LOL

Haute Couture, the second book in the Razzle My Dazzle series, is available now. Want a sneak peek? Turn the page for the exclusive peek!

Thank you again, from the bottom of my heart.

xo Joslyn Westbrook

HAUTE COUTURE SNEAK PEEK!

JAXSON

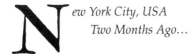 *ew York City, USA*
Two Months Ago...

"GETTING DUMPED ON NATIONAL TV IS WORSE THAN GETTING kicked in the fucking balls." I flash an innocent smile at the ladies sitting around the table, and the studio audience goes wild.

I'm on the set of *The Scoop*, talking to the hosts about my stint on the popular reality TV show called *Date Me, Then Marry Me*.

The show that basically ruined my life.

You see, I joined the cast of *Date Me, Then Marry Me*, hoping to find true love.

Okay. Hold on…

Before the jury gets reeled in for a judgmental *you're-an-idiot* verdict, let the record show I knew the odds of finding true love on a nationally televised reality show were slim-to-none. But, after being named the nation's most eligible bachelor by *Alpha Male Magazine*, women were literally throwing themselves at me.

Sure, it was a thrill ride.

For a while.

I mean having women galore? That shit fed my ego like it was some ravenous VIP at a Las Vegas buffet.

Yet, the rocket-boosted thrill ride crashed just as soon it set off. One-night stands left me feeling empty.

I wanted to find true love.

When the producers of *Date Me, Then Marry Me* contacted my agent, requesting I'd be their star contestant, I was more than ready to meet my future wife on a show that boasted a ninety-five percent success rate. A success rate that was far greater than the failure rate I had, trying to find a wife on my own. Dating apps like *Happn, Tinder*, and *OKCupid*, proved not to be cut out for a celebrity-type like me—even though Hollywood viewed me as a mere B-list actor. Besides, at thirty-two, I had enough of the typical dating scene. None of the women I was meeting were working out and regardless if it was them or me, I needed to find a different method of meeting Ms. Right for Jaxson Malone.

With that in mind, I gladly accepted *Date Me's* offer to be on the show which meant for six weeks, I had to live in Atlanta, Georgia—the show's filming location.

I was presented with thirteen amazing—fine as hell— women to date. Doctors, lawyers, teachers, entrepreneurs, and a sultry southern belle model, actress named Dixie Lane.

Damn. Even her name was *everything*. Not to mention it's always been hard for me to resist a southern belle—something about that southern drawl that sucks me in like a storm drain during a flood.

The platinum-blond-haired, green-eyed fox stood out from the pack in every possible way: confident, poised.

I did say sexy, right?

Having the same interests and the same career paths, the two of us were like fine wine and cheese—perfectly paired.

Even the show's three-million viewers dubbed us The

Perfect Couple. Why she decided to dump me, after a romantic dinner on the beach in front of millions of viewers on National TV, was beyond me.

When I got down on bended knee with that twinkling five-carat Harry Winston I was eagerly waiting to slide on her finger, her standing before me with the light breeze whipping through her long curly hair—believe me, the last thing I expected Dixie Lane to say right then and there was, "Um no. Just no," before she fled the set, like a fugitive chasing freedom.

Dumbfounded and rightfully wretched by The Ultimate Jilt, I was left there—just me, the rhythmic crash of waves sounding off in the distance, the orange glimmered sunset, that damn ring, the jaw-dropped camera crew, and Dixie's rejection spilling into the atmosphere like a fucked-up stink bomb.

Devastation washed over me like a tidal wave, its force crushing my heart and my elation of finding a wife.

To make matters worse, TV viewers practically broke Twitter as #UmNoJustNo went viral with over two-million tweets.

Two. Million. Tweets.

Of course, news of the *Um No Just No* jilt spread like an out-of-control wildfire with headlined captions: *Wait. What?*; *Oh No She Didn't!*; *Come Back Dixie, Come Back!*; and *Jaxson is Still Single, Ladies.*

I hated Dixie Lane for making a mockery of my love for her.

Weeks went by as I took shelter in my New York City apartment, unsuccessfully avoiding the media. Hastily, I agreed to one on-camera interview with the popular morning news show, *Wake Up America*—hoping to squash the media's desire to stalk me like ravenous wolves tailing their prey. And after explaining, on National TV, just how shocked, heartbroken, and emotionally bruised I was after the rejection, Dixie

Lane surfaced on the cover of *Superstar Magazine*, looking hotter than ever, her infectious smile taunting me, as she nestled snug in the arms of *Date Me, Then Marry Me's* lead cameraman. Apparently, the lovebirds were newly engaged.

Dixie was getting *married*.

Yep. It sucked to be me…

So, I did what any man in my position would have done. I decided to come on this show to tell the tenacious ladies of *The Scoop* and all of America the truth about Dixie Lane.

"Did you suspect she was seeing the hot cameraman? Like, did they ever exchange flirty looks?" asks one of the cohosts, the one who has a determined look practically living on her face.

"Uh. Nope. But it made me realize Dixie Lane was never on *Date Me, Then Marry Me* seeking true love." I turn my head to look directly into the camera, "Let's just say Dixie was on a mission to boost her lackluster modeling career."

The audience gasps. And the ladies around the table produce a varied mix of the ultimate *surprise* face.

"So, tell us," slurs the lead host as she sips on what I suspect is a little more than water, "what does the newly single Jaxson Malone plan to do now?"

I lean back in my seat, rub the stubble on my chin, and produce a smug shrug. "Disappear."

WANT TO READ MORE?

Haute Couture is FREE in Kindle Unlimited!

Click Here to download or purchase your copy of Haute Couture from Amazon.

ACKNOWLEDGMENTS

OMG - where do I even begin? There are so many behind the scenes stuff that takes place before the book is released to the world. So my acknowledgements are from the book's infancy to when it is born and ready for the world:

I have to thank the 405 freeway in Los Angeles for allowing me endless hours of sitting in traffic to be able to come up with book ideas and character concepts - LOL.

Thanks to my Cover Designer for the fabulous cover - I always seem to need the cover first before I dive into writing.

Thanks to Ashli and Vanessa for reading the book, one chapter at a time, providing feedback all along the way - I honestly do not think you two know how helpful you have been and the huge difference it makes when you offer feedback. LOVE YOU BOTH (yes, you are my daughters, but still…haha).

Jessica my dear, let me know when you want to join the party ;-),

Thank you to all of my author friends who continue to support me in this journey. Our conversations (even if only on Facebook messenger) are so helpful and at times SO needed when I need to rant or shoot off an idea that I feel needs tweaking. Maria, Roberta, Julie—you are all rock stars!! XO

My Editor...I mean, how FAB is she?! Kathy you have no idea how valued you are and how I SO appreciate you coming through for me on such a tight deadline to help make this book shine. You are beyond amazing and at times I wish I could just hug you (not in a creepy way, haha). THANK YOU!!!

Roberta - You came through when I thought I wasn't going to have a proofreader and I mean OMG you have NO idea how helpful you were!!! I owe you lunch whenever I make it to Milan. THANK YOU!!!

Tandy - Thank you again for being that final proofreader - you are a gem!

My Hubby - I LOVE YOU - thank you for listening to all of my writing woos, supporting me when I am stressed, and thank you for reading chapters and offering "guy talk" guidance. You are not just prince charming-ish—you are the real deal. My Prince Charming. XOXO

ARC Team - I know I got this to you later than desired!! So sorry!! Thank you all for your last minute feedback and as always, thank you for taking time out of your busy lives to read the ARC.

XO Joslyn

ABOUT JOSLYN

Wife. Mom. Foodie. Fashion Junkie. RomCom Lover.

Author of romantic comedies and contemporary romance, Joslyn Westbrook's novels feature strong, sassy, female heroines and the alpha-swoontastic heroes who sweep them off their feet.

When she's not writing, Joslyn can be found binge-watching Netflix, cooking, shopping, and spending time with her husband and children in sunny California.

You can connect with Joslyn via the links below:

CPSIA information can be obtained
at www.ICGtesting.com
Printed in the USA
FSHW020149101019
62789FS

9 780692 905814